blessed

ACADEMY OF THE SERAPH

BOOK ONE
blessed

BOOK TWO
captured

BOOK THREE
broken

blessed
academy of the seraph

BRANDI ELLEDGE

The characters and events portrayed in this book are products of the author's imagination and are used fictitiously. Any similarity to real persons, living or dead, is coincidental and not intended by the author.

Printed by Ann James Publishing, June 2020
Copyright © Brandi Elledge, 2020
WWW.BRANDIELLEDGE.COM

Cover and interior design by We Got You Covered Book Design
WWW.WEGOTYOUCOVEREDBOOKDESIGN.COM

All rights reserved. Unauthorized distribution or reproduction is strictly prohibited without the express written permission of the publisher.

ISBN: 978-0-9967193-3-9

To the queen, the ride-or-die, the heart of the family, my mama.

I can't imagine anyone ever loving me as much as you do. You have always been my biggest fan and the first person I run to when I've had a bad day. You get me. Also, I love how you kick people out of the village without even asking me.

Daddy might guard the village but girl you run it.

prologue

EVERY ANGEL WHO SAT AT the round table was grieving. All fifteen of them had invested something in humanity and hated to see what they thought of as their children suffering. They all had been instructed to do nothing, but the cries of the mortals hurt their souls.

An unstoppable disease burned through the land. It didn't stop for the young or old, the strong or weak. It spread wide with an unforgiving vengeance.

Fifteen angels had gathered to comfort each other. They were the mighty archangels. The ones who were the defenders, and yet they were unable to defend the weak ones. The humans.

Azrael was the first one to speak. "Is there anything we can do?"

Haniel sighed. She was weary to the bone. Her wiry,

orange hair swayed as she shook her head. "We have been instructed not to interfere with the dying."

"Then we mustn't," Jeremiel added, his ebony face filled with regret.

"Mustn't we?" Beautiful Ariel began to pace with her lioness stride. "Yes, we have been taught to obey, but also to think. It's not *if* they will all die; it is *when*."

Michael, who was never one for words, grunted. He hated to talk unless someone directly asked him a question that required an immediate answer.

He sat reclined back in his chair, his masculine form taking up a lot of space. He ran long fingers through his sandy blond hair as he listened to his brothers' and sisters' murmurs.

Jophiel, who was beautiful in her own quiet way, watched her sister, Ariel, pace the floors in their heavenly chambers. Finally, she couldn't take it any longer and said, "Ariel, if you have a suggestion, let us hear it."

Her blue eyes twinkled. "What if we give a select few a gift before they go?"

Metatron scoffed. "What gift could a human need when on death's door?"

Azrael caught her line of thinking quicker than the others. "You wish to heal them?"

"I realize," Ariel began, "that being the angel of death, this would war the most with you, Azrael, but please hear me out. They cry for our help, and soon, there will be nothing left of them. We the defenders could give them another chance at life." Tears streamed down her porcelain face. "Please, brothers and sisters."

Murmurs erupted, but Metatron quieted everyone down. If there was anyone who would understand Ariel's need to save the humans, even if it was but a few, it would be Metatron, because once upon a time, he had also been human.

When he spoke, his voice was full of empathy. "Ariel, first of all, any we bless would remain that way. Generation after generation, they would have something a little extra and—"

"I understand the ramifications." Seeing that she had at least one of her brothers' and sisters' attention, she hurriedly continued, "Answer me this, brother; do you think it was a coincidence that this plague happened so closely after Lucifer and the other angels fell from grace? This is no coincidence. We are supposed to be defenders. Let us defend. Don't let the fallen, the darken, win."

Raguel, the logical one of the bunch, sat back as the other angels talked over one another. "Who would we choose to save? It should not be our decision who lives or dies."

Ariel wet her lips. "What if we blessed those who showed some sort of heroism during the battle of all this death that is warring down upon them?"

"There would have to be rules," Raziel said. He seemed always to know the correct answer. "If there were rules in place, then perhaps we could justify our actions."

Metatron's twin, Sandalphon, who was the tallest of all angels, stood from the table. He was stunningly attractive and, just like his brother, every part of him looked like he was handcrafted to perfection. The only difference was Metatron was shorter and his build was less muscular.

Sandalphon said, "This could backfire on us."

"But …?" Ariel asked hopefully.

Sandalphon sighed. "But I think we should do something." He turned to Raziel. "These rules you speak of, do you have suggestions?"

Raziel shrugged his massive shoulders. "I could come up with a few."

Uriel asked, "How about we figure it out as we go?"

"Tonight," Raziel added. Ariel started to speak, but he held up a hand, stopping her. "Sometimes, it's better to ask for forgiveness than permission. We have one night to heal as many as possible. Then we all agree that we're done. No more interference from us."

Ariel leaned a shoulder against a column. Sweet, sympathetic Zadkiel went over to her and rubbed her back. He knew that if Ariel had it her way, she would drain herself to a husk in order to save as many as she could.

Gabriel, who had been quiet this whole time, tossed her long mane of brown hair behind her shoulders. Her ethereal beauty was beyond compare and as bright as her positive attitude.

Never one to be discouraging, she had decided to remain quiet and let the others determine the fate of the humans, but when she saw that they were all quickly agreeing to Ariel's plan, she said, "I think it is a wonderful thing you speak of, Ariel, but what if these humans end up hating us?"

Ariel shook her head. "How could they hate us for saving them? No, we go tonight."

Gabriel sighed heavily when she saw she was losing the battle. She had many attributes, and one of them was her foresight.

She quietly asked, "How far are all of you willing to go? Would you still save the humans if it meant your death?"

They all agreed, except for Sandalphon, who had been watching her keenly. She refused to meet his eyes in fear that he would see the truth.

After a few more minutes of discussing whom the angels would be looking for, they separated into groups of two, except for the last group, who would be made up of Ariel, Gabriel, and Sandalphon. Then the angels went off, seeking those who had formidable traits—warriors amongst the humans.

It would have all gone as planned, except that none of them had known that there had been an angel spying on them. One who wanted nothing more than to bring the archangels themselves to their knees.

one

IT WAS TESTING DAY, THE day I had feared for more than a year now. Sixteen was the age in which all the touched or blessed, who I personally called "the infected," were hunted down and made to enroll at one of the two academies—the Academy of Seraph or Empowered Academy. Recruiters from both academies went near and far to find any of the blessed. The Academy of Seraph had a formal way of finding us. The Empowered Academy sent darken out to find us on the streets. Another reason I rarely left whatever home I was currently residing at—you never knew what came out at night, or daylight, for that matter.

Those who had been blessed by any of the fifteen archangels were called demis. If you had been touched by an archangel *and* a fallen angel, also known as the darken, then you got labeled as a "fully blessed." In my opinion, either way, you were screwed. Being straight-up human was the way to go.

It usually wasn't until puberty when we started to show signs of being blessed, so they usually left us alone until sixteen—or, at least sixteen was supposed to be the age.

Thanks to me being a recluse and being rehomed several times, I had successfully avoided six tests and had dodged my fate for almost two years. I had hoped to avoid this one, as well, but my new foster parent had received a letter from the Academy of Seraph in the mail saying I had been flagged, and they expected to see me at the next testing no matter the circumstances. No one wanted an angel showing up on their doorstep, so my foster parent reminded me a hundred times last night that I was to go to the testing.

Bouncing around from foster home after foster home had taught me how to pretend, and it helped that I was never in one place long enough for anyone to notice anything abnormal. However, if I didn't show up for the testing day, it would be a huge red flag, and they would send someone after me.

Sometimes, I wondered what America used to look like before the angels went to war amongst each other. It didn't look like a warzone ... yet, but there were parts in every county, in every state, that had been affected by the angels. Vindictive angels could do a lot of damage in a little amount of time.

In the beginning, the archangels had tried their hardest

to keep a tight lid on everything, but the darken and their demons didn't care if humans knew they existed. In fact, they preferred it—at least that way they got to see their fear.

Ever since the last decade, the angels had been playing a game of sorts. Kind of like capture the flag, but with blessed as their prize. Anyone who tested positive for the "abnormal" gene was sent to one of the academies. The Academy of Seraph was formally testing in my neighborhood today. If they found out who I really was, well, truth be known, I could do a lot worse. It was said that the Empowered Academy fought for the darken and had been known to bring students in line with their torture tactics.

All of it was a moot point because I didn't want to be a part of any of it.

I had been having dreams since I was twelve years old. Not a princess being rescued out of a castle dreams, but dreams of kids killing kids in a war that they shouldn't have inherited. If I had one wish, it would be to be human. But that wasn't the case. So, what did I do? I dodged the testings and pushed down that power that was usually humming inside of me when I must leave the house, prolonging the inevitable for as long as I could.

The testings held by the Academy of Seraph were held at schools, private and public. Home schoolers got visited.

I had tried for years to find out exactly how they tested us, but the problem with that was no one knew. Once you tested positive, you were taken. I would figure out a way to make sure that didn't happen to me, though.

I tied my long, brown hair in a ponytail, grabbed my faded backpack, and then headed for Saint's Christian School, where I was currently enrolled. I had never witnessed testing before, but I was sure everything was going to be all right. This was going to be no big deal. Maybe it would be a survey of sorts. If you thought you held an abnormal gene, then check the box kind of thing. I would draw little hearts above my name and giggle as I filled out the form, underlining that there was absolutely nothing in the world wrong with me, and *bada-bing, bada-boom*, I'd be scot-free. I laughed at the absurdity of that.

The trees blew in the wind, as if they were trying to reach out their branches toward me. I hunched my shoulders and pretended that I didn't notice. If I told anyone that, for the last six months, trees tried to embrace me, they would think I was crazy or know I was blessed. Honestly, I'd rather them think the first.

A dog was barking crazily as I rounded the corner. I froze in my tracks when I saw it laying on the porch. I met his brown eyes, and my stomach twisted. I started to just walk away, but I couldn't bear the thought of him suffering.

Mrs. Harrington was in her pillowcase dress, watering her roses. She was half-crazy, so would she recognize someone who was touched with a little craziness herself? Doubtful. I hefted my backpack higher my shoulder. There was only one way to find out.

"Hi, Mrs. Harrington," I called.

"Hello, Gabriella."

"Um …" I looked at the old hound dog again. "So, I read an article that the mosquitoes were really bad this season and a lot of dogs were being infected, causing them to have heartworms. I think you should get Blue tested."

Mrs. Harrington looked to where the hound was laying. "You think so?"

"Definitely. He looks like he might not be feeling well."

"You know, he has been acting strange. I'll call the vet today."

I gave her a warm smile. "Sounds good."

She shook a skinny finger in my face. "I just heard on the police scanner that there was demon activity at the mall last night. A pretty girl like yourself can't be too careful. Maybe you should stay away from the mall for a while."

I had no money to spend, so that would be super easy. "Yes, ma'am."

"Those demons are spreading out of their territory. It'll start with a couple, and then the next thing you know, *bam*, they will be everywhere, causing damage like a tornado in flat plains."

"Yep. Well, I better be off, or I'll be late."

She gave me a curt nod, and I cast one last glance at the hound before I continued on to school. I shouldn't have stopped, but the damn dog was in pain and suffering. I was infected, which was normally a curse, but sometimes it had its blessings. If Mrs. Harrington called the vet and got

Blue fixed, then at least I could say what's going on with me was not all bad.

Two minutes of brisk walking and I entered the back of the auditorium. I found a seat next to a pudgy kid named Jake. He was super nice, and I wasn't just saying that because he sometimes brought me homemade cupcakes that his mom baked.

Jake's face lit up when he saw me. He started rambling about the football game coming up this Friday while kids were filing into the auditorium. Apparently, it was homecoming, and there would be a bonfire afterward. Like I had time to care about things as trivial as after-school parties.

I took a deep breath. If habitual liars could pass lie detector tests, I could pass one silly little testing.

The principal stood up and made his way to the stage. "Students, I know everyone is excited about today, but please keep the chatter to a bare minimum. This shouldn't take too long, but it will help to speed up the process if each of you listens for your name." He waved for someone who was standing off to the side to come onto the stage.

The man was perhaps twenty-one, but the way he moved told a different story. He didn't just walk onto the stage; he moved with an athletic grace that should have been impossible for someone with his large frame.

With every step he took, the auditorium grew quieter. Whoever this man was, his presence was domineering. I could see the definition of his muscles poking out under his T-shirt, and I was in the back row. Maybe he was one of the fully blessed? Whatever he was, he was drop-dead gorgeous with his jet-black hair and piercing green eyes.

"This is Finn Martinez," the principal introduced. "He is the commander of the academy that will be testing you today."

As the commander roamed his striking eyes around the crowd with a predatory gaze, I slouched down in my seat with fear that he would be able to somehow read something on my face. I wasn't a fantastic liar, but I was confident that I would be able to answer the appropriate questions asked at the testing in order to avoid going to the academy. I just had to quit freaking out so badly.

His voice was deep and sexy as he addressed the crowd. I even heard a couple of girls sigh.

"As your principal said, I'm the commander for the Academy of Seraph. This should go smoothly. I need to be very clear on what we are looking for today. A student must carry at least a tenth of the angel gene in them before they can be admitted to the academy. However, that does not mean that they will be able to join the army after graduating. If the student is deemed warrior material, then they will be given a job. If they are not a fit for the army, they will be returned home. We will begin right away."

My knee jerked up and down nervously. No need to worry just yet or plan an exit strategy. He was probably just going to ask a few questions then send us on our way.

Jake had pulled out his phone and was showing me his

new Instagram photo, but I was barely paying attention as names began to be called in alphabetical order. *Great.* Why did my last name have to start with an A? Apparently, they had a few recruits asking questions, because the names were being called faster than I had anticipated.

Jake said, "Wouldn't it be cool if we were touched? Like straight-up angel blessed."

Not at all. "Sure."

"You know, I heard that the demons are kicking asses and taking names."

I nodded. "Yeah, maybe that's why they have to test so frequently."

"Nah. They have to test because everyone in the county would be trying to say they are touched."

Nope. Not this girl. Totally inaccurate statement.

"Jake, you do realize that, if you get selected today, you will be fighting not only demons who are employed by the darken, but you will be at war with the other academy that trains their students to become darken."

Jake pointed at the commander who was on stage. "Look at that dude. Whatever side he's on is the side I want to be on. He probably eats demons for breakfast."

I rolled my eyes. "So, what do we do? Fill out a form, and if we think we're one of them, they run us through a more advanced test?"

He shrugged. "I guess." He leaned in close and whispered, "So, what do you think the fully blessed can do? I wonder if they can shoot laser beams from their eyes."

"Who knows?"

"Wouldn't it be my luck to be one of the blessed just to find out that I'm a demi whose blood is super diluted. Who am I kidding? I'll still take it. That's bragging rights."

"Even if you were touched by one of the darken?"

"The archangels fell, too. They just didn't get labeled as the bad guys. The way I see it is, an angel is an angel." He gave a wave over his body. "Don't I look like I come from an angel? I could so be a demi."

He was trying to make me laugh, but I wasn't in the mood. "You sure do. Man, I hope they hurry."

Jake gave me a weird look before he went back to playing on his phone. "Why hurry? We are getting out of algebra just for this, and if we're lucky, we will get out of history, too."

Finally, I heard my name. Gabriella Arien.

I gripped the armrest when my name was repeated.

Jake lightly elbowed me. "Hey, you're up."

"Yeah"—I laughed nervously—"I'm up."

When I walked up the stage, someone ushered me to the right. I wiped my sweaty palms on my pants again and made a pledge to myself to not do that thing I did when I was super nervous—rambling. Words would just spew out of me like I was possessed. But not today. Nope. Today, I refused to ramble. I was going to be cool. Chill. There was nothing to worry about. I had succeeded in dodging these fools for almost two years, and even though weird things happened around me, no one had made a connection that

I was infected yet. I had this.

With new confidence, I plastered on my best poker face as I was ushered to where a makeshift cubicle had been set up. Mr. Hottie himself gestured for me to step behind the walls. In all my life, I had never seen someone more handsome.

When his eyes met mine, I saw his body tense and his jaw clench as his eyes roamed all over my body. There was no way he knew what I was just by looking at me. I didn't even know what I was.

I began to sweat profusely as he stood there, just staring at me. I nervously straightened my flannel shirt. Were there holes in this one? Did I have syrup on my face?

He must have known he was staring, because he said, "I'm sorry." His voice was strained, almost like he was in pain. "I thought …" He cleared his throat. "Please, step over here." He looked as if he was forcing himself to relax, which made my anxiety rise.

There were several potted plants on the side of the stage lined up in a row that the theater teacher was using as props for *Where the Wild Things Grow*. The plants' leaves gently lifted as if a breeze was coming through, but I knew better. They were reaching for me.

I made sure to walk a little farther than he had suggested so his back was to the plants. If he thought I was odd, he didn't comment. He just took out a wand of sorts.

I immediately started to panic.

"What's that?"

His eyebrows went to his hairline as he studied me. "It's how we tell if someone has powers. Just hold still, and it'll be over in a second." He was curt and to the point, something I would have appreciated if I wasn't about to pee myself.

"Is it safe to use if I have metal in my body?" Maybe there was a way to get out of this. Where was the damn form I was supposed to fill out? This had to be a violation of some sort.

"Of course it's safe." He looked exasperated. "Do you have metal in your body?"

"No." My eyes immediately searched out the closest exit. "I was just wondering." I then closed my eyes and pushed the warm hum that I always felt throughout my body into a tight ball and mentally tried to hide it.

My eyes opened as the wand went over me slowly then lit up green.

The commander narrowed his eyes that turned greedy as he scanned over me just as the wand had done.

I crossed my arms over my chest. "Good news, huh? I passed." Nervously, I then said, "You know, green means go. Everybody knows that. Am I right, or am I right?" *Oh, gawd!* I was beginning to ramble more and more.

He talked into an earpiece that I hadn't seen before. He was all official-looking, and I was probably screwed.

"Have you possessed any powers or shown any signs of anything abnormal?" he asked.

"Nope, nothing, nada." Why couldn't I have just stopped

with nope? My lips parted before I could stop them. "Zilch."

"Are you sure?" He narrowed his eyes. "This makes no sense. Try to think. The abnormalities could even be something small that has happened, like having good intuition about people."

Oh, that was putting it mildly. I always knew when someone had ill intent. Also, I had that thing with animals, like I could perfectly communicate with them. Then there was the thing with plants and trees, and a couple of other little crazy things that happened to me or around me.

I bit my lip and frowned. "Yeah, there's nothing out of the ordinary happening with me. So unfortunate, too. It'd be cool to have superpowers, but that's a negative for me. I've never shown signs of being infected."

If possible, he stood taller, like a looming shadow over me. His green eyes bore into mine as if he was trying to read my mind. What if he could read my mind? What if that was his superpower?

Sweat dripped down my spine as I mentally pictured lots of unicorns eating tacos. If he was reading my mind, he was about to be confused as hell.

"Nothing, you say?"

I tapped a finger on my chin. I had theater for a whole month. I needed to tap into those limited acting skills like I was performing on Broadway. "I mean, I've got good intuition about people, but only because I'm a behavioral expert. Kidding. So kidding." I rocked back on my heels. *Don't try to be cute or funny and don't ramble. Just don't.*

"Seriously, I don't know what else to tell you. I've never shown any powers."

With his green eyes, he raked my body. "I'm sure. Sit down, please."

Oh shit. "Sure. No prob."

I sat in one of the two chairs as he turned his chair around, straddling it. He rested his chin on the back of the chair and just looked at me like he was studying me for an exam. With his hypnotic green eyes, he scanned my face like he was going to paint it later, or like he was reading me.

Little tacos danced in a perfect formation while unicorns pranced around, leaving glitter trails with their hooves. The plants behind him looked like a tropical storm had hit. I needed to calm the hell down. If he turned around, I was screwed.

I took a couple of deep breaths. I was going to be fine. For affect, I added a fake yawn. *Here's me being relaxed.*

"Are we about done here?"

"Testing days are exciting for most." He made a gesture to the surrounding makeshift cubicles. "All the ones being tested now, I can feel their excitement. They hope and pray that they are one of the blessed, even if they are a low percentile demi."

"Yeah, I bet." Not me. I had enough of those nightmares that might not add up too much but was enough to deter me away from anything heaven sent. Thanks, but no thanks.

He talked into his earpiece again, and then he sat there,

just staring at me, until a small red-headed girl came over and handed him a file.

My leg bounced up and down as he read the file. I caught a glimpse of a photo of me.

"Your birthday is on New Year's?"

"Yeah, so?" Oops, that might have been a little defensive. I tried to counterbalance it with a smile that showed a little too much teeth.

"It says here that you avoided the last several tests. Any reason why?"

"Avoided? Oh, I wouldn't use that word. That implies that I didn't want to be here. No, I just happened to be switching schools or was deathly sick on those dates." Never been sick a day in my life. "I mean, why would anyone want to avoid testing?"

He threw the folder onto the table. "You said earlier that you've never shown signs of being infected."

Shit. I laid a hand on my chest. "No, sir, I think you misheard. I said I've never shown signs of being blessed. The acoustics in this place aren't the best. There's not a lot of extra money for the school, but I love this place." *All six weeks that I've been here.* "Go, Titans!"

"You see, I don't think there is anything wrong with my hearing, and I know there is nothing wrong with the wand."

At his words, the salvia dried in my mouth.

He yelled for someone named Johnny to take over his post as he grabbed my elbow and tugged me out of my chair. At his touch, my body began to hum as a pleasant feeling began to crawl over me. I couldn't help looking up at him, seeing his jaw tighten. He didn't seem to be feeling what I was by his mere touch.

Somehow, my legs stayed under me as he walked me out of an exit door and toward a woman who had a small table set up outside of the school.

"You're taking me to the alley? What are you going to do? Shoot me?"

He grunted. "Don't be silly." He handed me over to the small-statured woman who was in her late forties. In this heat, her gray hair curled around her framed glasses.

The commander said, "Margaret, we have one of the *touched*"—he said the word slowly, as if to make a point—"whether she wants to admit it or not."

She gave me a friendly nod, even though she looked confused as to why I had to be forced to her table.

He pushed me down into a seat, his hand branding my shoulder. "And I think she's a runner, so be careful."

Everything was happening too fast.

"*Runner?* What would I be running from? You've been mistaken with your two-dollar, Wal-Mart, blowing-bubbles wand. I'm not blessed, infected, and definitely not touched. None of the above. I won't be checking any boxes here today, folks."

They both looked at me like I was crazy.

I took a deep breath. "Look, I think there has been a mistake."

The commander's green eyes held a touch of impatience. He leaned down so close to me that his lips skimmed my ear. "I have searched so long—" He abruptly stood up and faced Margaret. "Get her registered, please." Without waiting for me to say another word, he turned around and strolled back inside of the school.

It took several seconds before I could get my breathing under control. The commander was as hot as he was dangerous.

I took a deep breath as I faced my next obstacle. "Margaret, was it? What a beautifully old-fashioned name. So charming. And what a beautiful sunny day it is. Everything about today is just so great." I was spiraling out of control, but God help me, I couldn't shut up. "You know what would be great on such a hot day? Ice cream. There's a little shop down the way. What do you say I go get us a scoop?"

She laid a hand on my arm, stopping me from standing. "Child, it's eight thirty in the morning."

"Silly me. Coffee then?"

She gave me a comforting smile. "Everything is going to be okay." Her hand warmed over my arm as she closed her eyes. She made a humming sound in the back of her throat, and her body swayed to and fro as her eyelids fluttered, before they flew open in shock. "Yes, dear, they have been mistaken."

I smiled. "See?" I tried to stand again, but she didn't release me.

"You are way more powerful than the wand was letting on. It shouldn't have just turned green. Maybe orange or possibly red, but not green. Which makes me wonder exactly what you are." She frowned as she picked up my file. "Surely not blessed by the darken." Then she patted my hand. "Don't worry though, child. The commander gives even the darken blessed a chance at the academy."

"Look, lady. No offense, but you're crazy. You trust a cheap wand that lights up, and then you all"—I closed my eyes and swayed in my seat while moaning—"and then you're like, *yep, you're infected*, and you expect me to be like, *sure and thanks*? No. I want to talk to your manager. You know what? Never mind. I don't want to cause a scene or get you fired. Let's just put this behind us. You go your way, and I'll go mine."

Margaret sighed. "Child, it's not a bad thing to be touched. Not sure what you've heard, but you'll love the academy."

Heard? I'd heard nothing. But I had seen a helluva lot in my dreams about angels, and I wanted no part of that shit storm.

She slid a huge, white binder with the logo of black wings my way. "Take this and read up on it. You'll need to report to the school first thing tomorrow. You won't be able to enter the school by yourself, so we give out several addresses that you can choose from. Pick one and text the number on the back of the folder to let your guide know your estimated time of arrival. If you don't have adequate transportation, that's fine, too. The guide can pick you up from your house. If you don't show up, they will come for you. Sometimes, you just can't fight destiny."

I tilted my chin up in defiance as I snagged the stupid binder. This was my life. My choice. They had no right to force me to the Academy of Seraph. My destiny was not to get mixed up in that mess, and I would do everything in my power to avoid that arrogant commander and his stupid school.

two

MARGARET WAS CORRECT. I DIDN'T show up for classes the next day, or the next, and then henchmen showed up at my door.

Both men looked like The Rock impersonators, dressed in all black with matching sunglasses. One of the Rocks announced that their names were Dan and Richard. I filed the information away under "don't care." They gave me five minutes to pack my belongings, which was overkill, since I didn't have much.

"Boys, I need to use the restroom before we head out."

Both of the Rocks just stared at me.

"Okay, well, I'll just go take care of business."

I went into the small bathroom and turned on the bathroom fan to muffle the noise that I was sure to make by opening the window. Then I pulled myself out the window and looked down. It was a two-story jump, but due to being infected by the holy ones, I knew that whatever I potentially broke would heal quickly. It would still hurt like hell, but we all had to make sacrifices in life. A little pain wasn't going to deter me, yet it was still scary as shit.

I threw my duffel bag out the window. Maybe if I was lucky, I'd land on it, and it would break my fall. Then I took a deep breath and jumped, missing the bag by a good foot. The ground met me before I was ready, and the wind was knocked out of me as I lay there, thinking I was dying. Eventually, I rolled onto my knees to try to gracefully crawl toward the shrubs. If I could just lie down in the bushes for a second, play a little hide and seek until I caught my breath, I would be as good as new in a couple of minutes. Bet I could outrun the blockheads, too. In fact, as soon as I had air back in my lungs, I would run like the wind. It wasn't a great plan, but it was all I had.

I almost made it to the hedge when a size fourteen boot came into my peripheral vision. I ignored Bigfoot and crawled faster, ignoring the pain in my ribs.

Hands grabbed me under my arms and gently helped me to my feet.

I blew a leaf from my face as I squinted at one of the Rocks. "Hey, bud, didn't know you were coming outside."

He grunted. "Boss said you were a runner. I prepare."

Seriously? "Could you have not yelled *don't jump* or something?"

"Funnier this way." He pointed to the other Rock. "He

videos it."

I glared at them both. I wasn't going. No, they would have to kill me first.

I took a swing at the one who still had an arm on me, and I swear the dufus rolled his eyes.

He patted my head. "Sleep, child."

And damn it to hell, that was the last thing I remembered until I woke up on a plane where they sat on either side of me, squishing me with their beefy bodies.

As soon as I made eye contact with one of the beef heads, his eyes widened like he was scared I would jump from the plane.

I could not believe my luck had run out. I glared at everyone who made eye contact with me. Then I decided I would scream my head off. Surely, someone would come to my defense.

The slightly more intelligent one tapped my head again, and sleep hit me like a fist.

The next time I woke up, I was in the back of a car that was going down a gravel, one-lane road. Then the Rocks parked in a grassy parking lot where I saw a sign that read, "*National Park*." One of the Rocks exited the car and plucked me out of the back seat. I refused to make this easy for them.

I stopped walking, so the Rock started dragging me. My heels left trails in the dirt, but when that proved to be too difficult, he threw me over his shoulder, and we began to hike up a mountain. I sighed loudly as I realized we were definitely far from Virginia.

I slapped him on the back. "Hey, kidnapper, what are we doing? You don't look much like a sightseer."

He bounced me hard on his shoulder as the other Rock scouted ahead of us. "We go to the academy."

"The academy is in a national park? Besides, this is stupid. They made a mistake."

"No, the academy is hidden. And no mistake. Do you see trees? They not make mistake with you."

My head swiveled to the tall, scraggly trees. They looked like they were about to be uprooted as they leaned at an unnatural angle, but as soon as we passed, they straightened.

I dug my elbow into his back and propped my chin up. "Nah, bruh. That's on you. I have never seen trees do that before."

He just grunted.

"So, Dick, how long until we are there?"

"It is Richard."

"Semantics."

"Girly, want to sleep again?"

I kept my mouth shut after that.

After an hour hike, Tweedledee and Tweedledum cut off the trail and headed into the forest. The hair on my neck stood up as they got closer to where the air seemed to thin. Behind a huge boulder, the air was completely shimmery. The first Rock, Dan, walked toward the shimmery air and disappeared.

The other Rock set me on my feet. "Don't worry; if you not blessed, you won't go through. Then you can stay here and feed the wolves."

"Charming." That was the last thing I said before he tossed me toward the boulder.

I closed my eyes, waiting for the impact of me hitting the unmovable object, but it never happened. Instead, I fell through the air then, for the second time in one day, I hit the ground, landing right beside where the first Rock stood.

"Oh, and what, you couldn't break my fall?"

The muscular oaf just shrugged. "You call friend Dick."

"If the boot fits, you have to lace it up and wear it." I dusted myself off as the second Rock landed on his feet in front of me. "Oh, and speaking of Dick, here he comes now."

Dick glowered at me, so I gave him a wink. "Sugar, did you miss me?"

The second Rock, AKA Dick, hid a smile as he tossed my duffel bag to me, and then each of the Rocks grabbed me by my arms and started shuffling me forward.

Exactly twenty hours later, I stood with one duffel bag in front of the Academy of Seraph. It was designed to look heavenly, like paradise or the Garden of Eden, but I knew differently. The building was a gigantic chateau made of stone and bricks that sat on a vast amount of land. The landscape was probably the most amazing thing I'd ever seen, yet I refused to be impressed. This grand estate was all smoke and mirrors, in my opinion. I bet there were a ton of skeletons in the closets.

As we walked down the cobblestone path, I noticed the multitude of gardens surrounding the house. The floral scent carried all the way to where I stood.

One of the Rocks nudged me forward, and it took everything I had not to hiss at him like a feral cat. Just because I wasn't fighting right now didn't mean that I had given up hope. I would find a way to break out of this place. I just needed to keep my cool. Maybe learn everything about them that I could. Then I would run.

If there was one thing I was good at, it was surviving.

three

I KEPT MY HEAD HELD high as the Rocks ushered me across the campus. It was dark outside, so there weren't too many students strolling about. There were two girls on the same path as us who wrinkled up their nose at me, looking at me like I was scum. Maybe it was the dirt-stained clothing, or the grass stains on my face.

I gave them a nod, and their lips curled up in disgust. *Boo.* It looked like I wouldn't be winning Miss Congeniality. There went all my hopes and dreams.

We entered a building, then dumb and dumber took me to what seemed to be the school library. They handed me off to a familiar, handsome face that I had never wanted to see again.

The commander tilted his head at me in greeting. "I assume you had safe travels?"

"If being forced against your will to leave your current residency, board a plane, then take some kind of nature walk just to fall through a rabbit hole when your name is not Alice and you don't enjoy adventures, and then, to add more suffering, you have to deal with two boring bozos like the ones who escorted me here is considered safe, then yes, it was peachy."

He gave a sigh as he took my raggedy duffel from me. "You're not going to make this easy, are you?"

"Nope. And why should I?"

His green eyes traveled the length of me, as if he was looking for wear and tear. Seeming to be satisfied, he said, "Let me show you where you will be staying."

"But I don't want to stay here. You'd think angels would be big on the whole *free will* thing."

"We are big on free will. However, you are being extremely difficult."

"So, it's only free will if I operate the way you want me to operate? And *difficult*?" I screeched, causing a couple of students to stop in their tracks to look at the new kid.

His eyebrows rose at my tone. "Yes, difficult." He took a couple of steps closer to me until there was but a few inches between us. Oh great, the commander even smelled divine, but I wouldn't be fooled by a pretty face and matching smell.

I cocked my head back, so I could still see him.

"We started this school for a reason—to give hope and options for all demis who have enough power that will cause them to be hunted by the darken. We are here to help the fully blessed, too. They have to learn who they are, how to control their powers, and what choices they'll eventually have to make."

I rolled my eyes. "And the hell with free will, huh? What if we don't want to be any of the above? And what if the choices we want to make have nothing to do with this stupid school?"

"A girl I once knew was just as stubborn as you. I learned with her that sometimes you have to drop a matter for a little while then revisit, so I suggest we do that. Now, if you are done making a spectacle out of yourself, please follow me."

I looked around the library. He was right; there were a couple of students gawking.

Holding my shoulders back, I begrudgingly followed him as we exited the main building and took a small, paved path to a smaller brick one. We entered through double doors and went up a winding stairwell. I took my sweet-ass time as I clomped up the stairs.

"These are the dorms." He pushed open a door leading to a room that was tiny and basic but clean. I had lived in so much worse. He set my duffel bag at the end of a bed. Another twin bed was against the other wall. "You'll have a roommate."

I just nodded. I had bigger problems than who would be rooming with me.

He handed me an envelope. "In there, you'll find your

classes. They begin tomorrow. They were supposed to begin yesterday, but I guess you had some loose ends to tie up."

"Yep, that was it."

"Today, you should rest and try to adjust to what your new life will be like."

I snorted.

"Gabriella, I didn't make the rules, but I do have to enforce them. It's for your own good. You're not safe out there. Not if you have been blessed."

I wasn't safe here, either.

He gave an impatient sigh. "I read your file. Your complete file."

My eyes flashed to his. That was a major violation of privacy.

He held up a hand. "As commander and leader of the seraph army, it's my job to read everyone's file. I noticed that you've had a bit of a tragic past. You've bounced around from home to home. At least here, you'll have a constant."

"Until when?" I snarled. "I've heard things, you know." Not really, but I'd seen what the angels were capable of. "I might not know all the behind-the-scene happenings, but I know enough to understand that I'm not safe here." I tilted my chin up in defiance. "Tell me, when's the last time a demi or fully blessed enrolled at your academy just to die by someone from the rivaling academy? Last year? Last month? How about last week?"

His eyes turned to steel. I must've hit a nerve.

I glared at him with all the rage I could muster. "I'm here. Not of my own free will, but by your command."

His eyes flashed with anger. "Understood. But understand this, your room is four levels up. Unless you're immortal, if you jump out of this window, it will kill you."

Oh great, the Rocks, Dan and Dick, had shown him the video. That was a tad humiliating, but who cared? I didn't.

I glared right back at the handsome beast. "I don't have anything else to say to you. You're dismissed." I held the door open for him, and as soon as he cleared the threshold, I slammed it so fast it barely missed his heels.

I threw myself on my new bed in a fit of tears. When I had no more room to wallow in my own self-pity, I gave a merciful laugh. I, Gabriella Arien, had just dismissed the commander of the scariest, most feared academy in the world. I might be in murky water, but I had balls. Here was to hoping that my bravado kept me alive instead of getting me killed.

four

I ACCIDENTALLY FELL ASLEEP FROM exhaustion. It was rare to dream about the angels. Ninety percent of the time, I had dreams of myself in a different time. They were weird dreams of people whose faces were murky, but there was no doubt that they loved me. Those dreams were always discombobulated and left me feeling depressed. Then there were the dreams of the academies. One dream I was being tortured until my voice was hoarse. I begged and pleaded, but no one came to help me.

Tonight, though, I dreamed of fifteen beautiful angels who had good intentions but broke the rules. They came down from heaven with a plan, but before returning, they realized that their new enemies, the fallen, the darken, had decided to counterbalance all their efforts.

"How did Lucifer know what we had intended?" one of the

archangels whispered.

Gabriel shook out her beautiful, long hair behind her then began to rub her temples. She was always my favorite angel. There was something about her that was so comforting. "Because someone told the fallen our plans."

"I bet it was Camaella," Ariel said.

Camaella came around the corner and clapped her hands together. "Looks like you all have it figured out."

"Why would you betray us to the enemy?" Azrael asked.

I already knew the answer to that. I had seen in before. She was tired of the way things were being ran in Heaven. She hated the fifteen archangels. Gabriel's beauty, Jophiel's condescending smiles and, more than anything, the way Sandalphon had turned down her affection. Her heart still clenched every time he made eye contact with her. She had practically thrown herself at him, and what had he said in his not-so-gentle rebuff? Oh, yes, angels weren't made to feel love. Perfect Sandalphon had made it clear that he wouldn't be breaking the rules anytime soon. Except, he did. For the humans.

Camaella shrugged carelessly. "Who cares for the reasoning?"

Abbadona, the angel who had been in charge of the fallen angels and currently the fifteen archangels, was nearing. They could all tell by the atmospheric pressure change.

At the look of fear and horror on the archangels' faces, Camaella smiled. She hoped that the head angel of the seraphim would make them pay, just like he had with her friends, the ones who they now called the darken. She no longer cared if she fell, too, as long as the precious archangels were thrown out of heaven, as well.

Abbadona showed up at the gate in a ray of light so bright that the other angels had to cast their eyes downward. The head angel's long, blond hair blew behind him, as if it was caught in the wind. His light blue eyes widened as they settled on the angles before him.

"What have you done?"

Uriel's eyes shifted to his feet with shame, causing Camaella to smirk. She had never liked him, with his meek personality and soft-spoken voice, always praising those around him. Such a bore, acting like he was building up their self-esteem. Instead, Camaella knew Uriel was really judging them.

Abbadona circled the angels, stopping before Michael. Laying a hand on his shoulder, Abbadona closed his eyes and breathed in the smell of human scent. Then Abbadona took a step back, disappointment coloring his face. "What have you done? What have you all done?"

Gabriel shook her head. "We have disobeyed, and we will gladly expect whatever form of punishment you choose to hand out, but it's not what we have done that is concerning. It's what she has done," she said, pointing at Camaella, "that might damn us all."

The dream started to fade, and I was thankful.

An overwhelming sense of grief filled me. I wasn't sure what the angels had done, but I knew from the bottom of my heart that they were going to be punished to the extreme.

five

THE SOUND OF MY NEW prison opened. Then the door slammed shut, causing me to groan. If that wasn't enough of an assault, the lights switched on, causing me momentary blindness.

"Oh, girl, you look like shit."

I looked up to see a girl who looked like a tiny pixie stroll into my room. Her black hair was swept to one side. The left side was short compared to the right, considering her hair was cut at a sharp diagonal. The tips were dyed red. Her eyebrows were tweezed, perfectly showcasing her baby blues.

"Who are you?"

Her mouth dropped open. Then she started tap dancing on the floor. "She's talking to me. A girl like you can see a girl like me." She sang "A moment like this" while she did a couple of dance routines that made Fred Astaire look amateurish, then she plopped onto the other twin bed. "So, my name, you ask? It's Remariey. Call me Remy for short, doll face. So, talk to Mama and tell me what's got you looking like a hella mess. Was it a boy? Was it a hot boy? Eek. Tell me, err-thang."

"Um. Are you my roommate?"

"Duh. And just FYI, you are going to love me. Like, you are going to wonder at some point what you did pre-Remy."

Remy was super weird. But I liked weird.

"Well, I'm sure glad we got that all cleared up. And it's nice to see a friendly face. I saw a couple of girls in the courtyard who were staring daggers at me."

"Oh … em … gee. Do you want me to verbally bitch-slap them? I'm the queen of that, baby, so don't try to go after my crown. But I'll let you assist me from time to time." She crossed her ankles while she studied me. "Yes, I have a feeling this is going to be a dream team. Now, let me explain these bitches real quick. There are two academies that search for kids like us, right?"

I nodded.

"And recruits are recruits. It's all game, baby. And because it's a game, everyone wants to win. Until everyone knows exactly who you are and what you're capable of, they will see you as a threat. You could be a powerful fully blessed that could be a game changer, or an evil darken that hides under their beds to murder them while they sleep." She made a dramatical noise. "Regardless, you have to watch your back while you're here." She ran a manicured hand over the mattress that did not have any linens on it. "Let's start this everlasting relationship by you telling me why you have mascara on your face." Her cute nose turned up in the air like a German Shepard. "And do I smell heavenly cologne? Yum. Who's been in here?"

I pushed back the mess that was my hair. "Cologne? Oh, that must've been the commander."

Remy splayed a hand over her chest while fanning her face with the other hand. "No, you did not just say the hottest male to ever walk the earth was just in my room."

"Yep."

Remy studied me with a different appreciation. "Yeah, yeah, I see it now. If your hair was brushed, the mascara was off your face, and you didn't have that drool caked on your chin, you would be smoking hot."

I wiped my chin with my sleeve. "I might not be at my best right now."

Remy came to sit next to me. "Talk to Mama. Was it that masculine beast that smells divine?"

I shrugged. "He did have me brought here against my will. I don't want to be touched or blessed. I don't want to be a part of this world." A tear streaked down my face. "I have these horrible dreams."

Her eyes widened. "Oh ... em ... gee, you're a dream walker!"

"Um, yeah, I don't even know what that is."

"Interesting." She tapped a finger on her chin. "You can be all tight-lipped right now, but I can promise you that you will be telling me all your dirty secrets within a week, because people just can't resist me."

I wiped my nose with my sleeve. "I'm not being secretive. I just really don't know what the hell a dream walker is. I get vivid dreams; that's it."

She cocked her head to the side, her red tips swinging over a shoulder. "Hmm ... Your powers haven't manifested all the way yet, so you could be a dream walker. I don't know for sure, though. How about the verdict is out on that blessing?"

"Not a blessing. The dreams are horrible. More like a curse. So, what have you been diagnosed with—"

She burst out laughing. "Yeah, no one will be able to tell how much you hate anything touched by an angel. But I agree, enough with you. Back to me. Obviously, by just looking at this fabulous face and great body, you can tell I'm fully blessed. By the lovely Ariel herself." She batted her eyelashes. "But I mean, look at this bone structure. You can so tell I'm fully blessed, right?"

I laughed. "Definitely see it now."

"Of course you do. I'm thankful that whatever darken angel that got to me after Ariel did was obviously attractive, as well."

"You're so humble."

She rolled her blue eyes. "Maybe that's the bad trait the darken had—narcissism. Anyway, I always knew that I was fully something. I mean, anything this hot can't be a demi. I'm going to take a stab in the dark here and say you're fully blessed, too. Even with snot dripping out of your nose, you're gorgeous."

"I don't want to be blessed. I just want the hell away from this school. This isn't my war." I thought about something. "So, if I'm not strong enough, they will kick me out of the academy?"

"Yep." She narrowed her blue eyes as she wagged a finger in my face. "Girl, please don't tell me you are going to try to fail. What is back home that's so great that you are willing to throw in the towel so quickly?"

Nothing. I had nothing. "I just don't want to kill."

She shrugged. "Then don't, but I can guaran-damn-tee that if a demon is clawing at your throat, your tune will change."

"Maybe. But don't think for one second that the commander won't use the most powerful of the students to go and do his killing for him."

"I don't know the commander well enough to pass judgment on him, but of course the best of the academy will go out to hunt demons and the darken. It's a war, baby. All of us will eventually have to fight, but until then, just chill. Remember, whatever you are, you still have a choice if you want to become that person."

But would I? I hadn't had a choice in whether I came here or not.

"I know that there is a war raging on earth and the

humans are stuck in the middle, but I'd like to know more. Like how it started and when it'll end."

"And I promise we can go all Nancy Drew tomorrow. I solemnly swear as your new B.F.F. to get to the bottom of these mysteries, even if that means I have to tie up the commander and torture him. As your diva-in-arms, I will take one for the team by seducing him. Now, it's your first night here, so can we, like, not be all mopey? Especially since there is a ton of people here who need us to make fun of them because they are the worst." She pointed to the open closest and a hot pink flamingo cosmetic case. "There's my makeup bag. Grab it and get yourself cleaned up, and then we will go down to the mess hall, and I'll gossip with you about all the people that I loathe. I'm not really a people person, so that leaves a lot of potential for us. Let's have a little fun before Friday."

"What's Friday?"

She swiveled her head my way so fast that I thought she was going to break her neck. "Okkkurr, girl, someone must've dropped the ball on explaining orientation. So, the last Friday of each month is when any newbs, such as yourself, go to a welcoming orientation to learn more about who you are and what line you come from. It's your official first meet and greet. It's kind of a big deal."

I didn't plan on being here by Friday. "Gotcha. I'll mark it on my calendar."

"Ew, sarcasm. Me like." She flopped down on her unmade bed. "I'm out of energy. I pulled so many pranks on those nasty bitches in that room down the hall. It was hilarious but exhausting. You'll have to grab the bag and do your own makeup. Normally, I'd do it for you because I can do the best smoky eye, but I need a nappy."

I was smiling as I went in the bathroom to wash my face. When I exited the bathroom, I was met with snoring. I silently laughed at Remy, who was sprawled out on her bed. There was no way I was waking her up.

Smiling, I flipped the light switch and crawled into my bed.

Maybe I didn't want to be here. Maybe my future looked bleak. But one good thing was I had a kick-ass roommate who might help me escape, so not all was bad. I was a survivor, and I'd survive this, too.

SIX

LIKE A ZOMBIE, I ROLLED out of bed, finding a customized backpack and a stack of uniforms that had somehow managed to find their way into my room. I sifted through the bag. There were a couple of pants that were pleather. I ran a hand over the rubbery material. They had a million-dollar budget for gardens but couldn't afford real leather? I shuffled through the rest of the stack that consisted of half a dozen T-shirts in black and white with the academy logo on them. Did I want to conform? Nope. I'd thumb my nose at the world and wear my hand-me-downs. I refused to relinquish the last little bit of control I had over my life.

I was smirking as I shuffled myself to the dining hall. I could feel tons of eyes on me, and it wasn't my imagination that the hall had grown quieter. Without making eye

contact with any of the students, I snagged an apple and a banana then headed to the classes on my schedule. I wanted to ask Remy if she'd walk me to my first class, but she was still passed out and twitching like a puppy dreaming about chasing bunnies. It was super weird and mildly cute.

I hadn't given up hope, but I knew that every day that went by, it would be harder to escape. Therefore, today, I would casually scout my surroundings. Staying here wasn't an option. If what I had seen in some of my dreams about this place were true, I could possibly not make it out of here alive. My life hadn't necessarily been great before, but dammit, I had been living.

I sat in my first class of the day. All the students stared as I walked in. This wasn't my first rodeo. I had been the new kid multiple times. Sometimes, the students were welcoming, and sometimes, they were just asses. It looked like I was going to be dealing with asses. *Yay, me!*

I went straight for a seat in the back, ignoring all the eyes that clung to me like tacky glue. I sat down and faced the front, reading the words that were written on the dry erase board. "*Archangels 101.*"

I went from learning geometry, advanced science, and American history to this? It was a little jarring. Why did anyone need to know about the archangels in order to fight demons? And how the hell was I supposed to fight demons? Distract them with billowing trees in the middle of a battle? I was slowly building a steady list of "what the hells?" when it came to this school.

The teacher came in, wrote her name on the board, and then went right to teaching in a very monotone voice. She must've been at least eighty. She had short, white hair and saggy skin, the color of snow. Her voice droned on and on as she started listing the angels one by one.

I looked around to see if anyone else was struggling to pay attention. Not one person was asleep. Huh, overachievers.

"Gabriella? What is the answer to the question?"

I shook myself out of my thoughts in time to see that the entire class was staring at me, waiting for my response to Mrs. Fields' question.

Meeting her stony stare, I apologized, "I'm sorry, Mrs. Fields, I don't know the answer."

She pushed her glasses on top of her curly white hair and huffed. "Perhaps it's because you don't know the question."

I heard a couple of kids snicker, making my cheeks flush.

Before I could offer another awkward apology, the bell rang, saving me from further embarrassment. I let everyone file out of the classroom before standing.

Mrs. Fields had her back to me, cleaning the dry erase board. I didn't owe her an explanation for not being an attentive student. I wasn't here by choice, and her purposefully embarrassing me in front of the class was a douche move. I was hoping that one of the teachers would feel sorry enough for me and help me to escape. I seriously doubted it would be this one, but a girl had to try. I hefted my backpack on my shoulder and made my way to her desk.

With her back still to me, she said, "Miss Arien, do you have something to say to me, or are you going to just stand there all day?"

Excellent. The woman had eyes in the back of her head, and she had no intention of making this easier on me.

"Mrs. Fields, I just wanted to say—"

"I know what you are here to say, Gabriella, and I don't want, nor do I accept, your apology," she interrupted me. "If you want to make it up to me, how about you start paying attention in class and strive to actually understand why you're here?"

I actually wasn't here to apologize, but I decided not to anger the beast any more than I already had. "Mrs. Fields, today—"

The look on her face made me halt my explanation. She didn't care that I was here against my will. She didn't care that today was my first day.

I gave her a nod. "I will try my best from here on out."

She threw her eraser down, and with a malice that I didn't fully understand, she turned to face me. "In my class, trying your hardest means nothing to me. Do you understand? Some grow up with parents patting them on the back, saying, 'Well, you tried your hardest, and that's all that counts.' Out there in the real world, everyone gets a trophy, whether they deserve it or not. It doesn't work like that here. You will not get a high-five from me for trying, Gabriella; you will get a failing grade. Do I make myself clear?"

I clenched my jaw to keep from saying so many things that were hovering on the tip of my tongue. However, I took the high road and mumbled, "Yes, ma'am. Sorry."

"Tomorrow, make sure that you are dressed to code."

Turning on my heel, I walked out of my history class without so much as a glance back. I needed to get the hell out of this school. I just had to get along with everyone until I figured out a way to leave the academy. Where I'd run to, I hadn't a clue. No family and no money would present lots of problems, but I'd cross that bridge when I got to it. Right now, I needed to keep under the radar. That meant not drawing any unwanted attention to myself and keeping my eyes open for an escape.

I looked at my watch to see I had four minutes until the next bell rang, and I had no clue where the gymnasium was located.

Lost in my own thoughts, I accidentally bumped shoulders with a pretty blonde girl. She was one of the two that I had first seen upon my arrival. Straight, blonde hair cupped her chin in a perfect bob, and her blue eyes danced with delight, as if she enjoyed us colliding with one another. Forget the standardized T-shirt, she was wearing an academy sweater with the school colors of white and black. She was obviously proud to be here. You'd never catch me wearing the school merchandise.

I went to offer my second apology of the day but was cut off with her loud clapping.

Her voice rose high in the crowded hall. "Can I have everyone's attention, please? Not only does the new girl smell of sour laundry and dresses like she is the proud owner of a secondhand shop, but she is also clumsy. Please, for everyone's safety, if you see her heading in your direction, move to the other side of the hall to avoid injuries and, of course, the horrible stench."

The crowd who had now gathered to bear witness to the embarrassing encounter started laughing.

Trying to avoid further torment, I put my head down and began to go around the evil chick when a beefy boy with a broad face said, "Hey, I would still tap that!"

I swiveled my head toward him as I gave him the same look the blonde girl was currently dishing out. My eyes were slits. These people disgusted me.

Seething, the girl asked, "Oh really, Devon? Since when is picking up an incurable disease on your top ten list?"

Devon slung an arm around the girl. "Oh, come on, Marlie-Beth. Don't go all dragon queen on me. You know that there is only one girl for me."

I darted my eyes away from them when they leaned into each other for a kiss, in fear that I might make my day even worse by throwing up from their gross public display of affection.

Just when I thought I was out of the range of fire and my humiliation might be coming to an end, another girl pushed me from behind, causing Marlie-Beth to snicker. I turned around to see a girl with curly, dirty-blonde hair in a high ponytail, her eyes glistening with hatred, an emotion that had my brow furrowing.

Oh, goody, it was the other girl who had sneered at me last night, and it looked as if they were besties and had decided to prove their friendship by being nasty to me. *Yay, for me.*

"Don't you have somewhere to go, skank?" she shouted while pointing at me, just in case anyone was confused about whom she was referring to.

Marlie-Beth high-fived the girl. "Angelina, you're so funny."

I rolled my eyes. "Totes. Like, lol."

They both glared at me. Obviously, they didn't think I was funny. Shame.

I didn't know how Mrs. Fields didn't hear the commotion going on out in the hall, but I was thankful she hadn't come out to add to my embarrassment.

Marlie-Beth balled up her fist, and it didn't take a psychic to know she was just warming up. She planned on putting on a show for the students.

I took a deep breath. I had never been in a fight before. This should be at least mildly interesting.

Suddenly, a stranger who stood a good head taller than everyone else in the gathered hall started breaking through the crowd, pushing students left and right. At first glimpse, the boy looked a little old to be a first-year resident. My guess was he was nineteen. He was hella hot with shaggy brown hair and big brown eyes. There wasn't an ounce of fat to him, just long, chiseled muscles. By the size of him, he was probably infected or, as the commander liked to say, fully blessed by someone grand. This was just great. He probably wanted his turn to humiliate me, as well.

I tilted up my chin, giving him my best "bring it on" look as I waited for his assault on my character, too. So, I was a little taken aback when he went right past me and stepped between Angelina and me with his back to me. Um, well, this was unexpected. What was I supposed to do?

He stood there in front of me, totally blocking my view of Angelina, but I could still hear her purr, "Why, hello, handsome." She elbowed Marlie-Beth. "We have another newbie."

I tried not to gag.

He just stood there, completely silent.

The other kids standing around started looking at each other with a question in their eyes. The same question that I was asking myself. *What's going on?*

After a long, awkward silence from all parties involved, the stranger turned to me and said in the sexiest southern drawl, "Come on, beautiful; I'll walk you to your class." Grabbing me by my arm, he forced me out of the circle of gathered students.

We walked a couple of steps before Angelina yelled at our retreating backs, "Be careful; she might be contagious."

Still dragging me along beside him, the stranger said loudly for all to hear, "I'll take my chances."

I couldn't help the smile that crept up my face. "Thanks."

The stranger had just saved me from getting my ass kicked.

"So, upon my arrival last night, I heard those students back there actually give their little group of friends a name. They labeled themselves *the crew*."

"You're joking, right?"

"Unfortunately, no."

"Well, that's entertaining, if not overwhelmingly pathetic at the same time."

The cute boy laughed. "Agreed."

"What gives them the right to act the way they do?"

"My best guess is they are fully blessed."

"Well, their darken side is showing." I looked over at him. "So, they think they rule the school, huh?"

His scan of me made me blush. "I guess they miscalculated that one, huh? Give it a week. I have a feeling you're going to be queen of the castle."

"Just a hunch, huh?"

He gave me the cutest grin. In return, one lit my face as we walked outside toward a building that was located at the corner of the U-shaped architecture. I was still trying to wrap my brain around what had happened back there.

Thanks to being touched or blessed—whatever they were labeling me as—I'd always been able to read people. Marlie-Beth and Angelina hated me, and I wasn't talking about can't stand onions on my hot dog kind of hate. I was talking loathing. I had a bad feeling that the other newbie had just put himself in that group's crosshairs by defending me. Maybe he didn't truly understand the ramifications of his actions.

"You know that group might cause a lot of trouble for you."

He smiled down at me. "Since when does the devil not know trouble?"

I admired his attitude. "What's your name?"

He dropped his hand from my arm, and I immediately missed the warmth. "Trev, and I got to tell you, I thought today was going to be a real bust." He gave me a half-smile. "But it's starting to look up."

I laughed. "Yeah, well, I personally think today still sucks."

He skimmed my body with his eyes. "Maybe you're not viewing what I'm seeing."

Oh, he was a flirt, and a good one.

The bell rang and I stopped walking. "I've made you late. Really, I can walk myself to hand-to-hand training."

He put a hand on my back and steered me down the narrow hall. "Trying to get rid of me already? First of all, I said I was going to walk you. Secondly, I'm the new kid. What teacher is going to scream at me if I said I got lost on my first day of school? And last but not least, it just so happens that my second class of the day is hand-to-hand training, too."

I seriously doubted this guy was lost. After all, he was leading me.

"So, how come you're just now enrolled at the academy?" He looked at least three years older than the recruiting age of sixteen.

He gave me a smirk. "How come you're just now enrolling?"

That was fair. "I guess life got in the way." There was no way I was admitting to anyone that I had dodged the testing. I needed to keep a low profile.

"Yeah, I reckon that's my reasoning, too."

I had a feeling he was lying just as much as I was, but I sure as hell wasn't going to call him out on it.

It was on the tip of my tongue to ask him what he was, but I hesitated. That might be a rude question. Truth was this was all new territory to me. I wasn't sure what topics were taboo.

"What's your name, beautiful?"

"Gabriella."

He took all of me in again. "That fits."

Stopping at our classroom door, he made a motion for me to go before him. "Ladies first." We walked into the gymnasium, where everyone was milling about.

Before I could head to the girls' locker room, Trev said, "You know why that group was singling you out, don't you? Jealousy. You're gorgeous—"

"From what I've seen, most of the blessed are more than moderately attractive."

He shrugged. "Some more than others. And"—he leaned in to smell me—"you are either suppressing your powers or you're weak."

"Um, thanks?"

He laughed. "Girls like them are going to assume that you're just hiding your powers, and they'll be out for blood."

I thought about the power I had on lockdown since even before the commander had took a wand to me.

Looking him in the eye, I said, "I'm not hiding anything."

I liked Trev, but I wasn't ready to show anyone my cards yet. Those girls would eventually see how unimpressed I was with the academy, and once they realized how little I cared to be here, they'd back off.

Hopefully.

seven

TREV AND I EXITED THE locker rooms at about the same time. He gave me an appreciative look before he let out a low whistle, causing me to blush. This was almost as embarrassing as my almost fist fight. The gym clothes, if you could even call them that, were more like scraps of cloth. Trev's attire was like all the other boys in the class—black T-shirt and tight shorts like what MMA fighters wore. Girls wore sports bras and tiny shorts that must have been called booty shorts, because nothing should be so little. Supposedly, the outfit was designed to allow free movement without the clothes restraining our motions. Whatever. I was modest and couldn't help but tug on the shorts every five seconds.

All the students were gathered in a circle around a wrestling mat. Trev made room for us between two kids.

I would have preferred to be on the outside of the circle, but oh well.

"It looks like we have a few new students. I'm Mr. Montgomery, and what are your names?" he asked.

I stared at our teacher, who was in his mid-forties, muscles galore, and slightly balding, and found myself the center of attention.

Trev cleared his throat and saved me from all the questioning eyes by saying in his dripping honey voice, "I'm Trev Butler. I just got here late yesterday from South Georgia, and this is Gabriella." He put a hand on the small of my back while he smiled down at me. My skin tingled in response. A smile came upon his face, as if he knew exactly what his touch had done to me.

It was so quiet in that gym that you could have heard a pin drop as Trev just stood there, smiling down at me. I felt myself blushing all the way to the roots of my hair.

Mr. Montgomery nodded. "Welcome. Okay, students, you are all grouped in this class for one reason. You are either new here or your powers haven't come to the surface yet, which means we're not sure what powers you can wield. So, until then, we will be learning some basic combat skills.

"As of right now, you will learn the basics of fighting without weapons. Classes here are not like normal classes. Once you've mastered the requirements, then you will be switched to a harder class."

He slapped his hands together. "Now, today in class, we

have a special treat. The commander has come to watch and possibly train with you. This is a huge honor, so I expect each of you to be on your best behavior."

I groaned as the commander made his way out onto the mat. His green eyes raked the crowd, landing on me for a few seconds, before he continued scanning the remainder of the students. Wouldn't you know it, Mr. High and Mighty didn't have to wear these ridiculously tight outfits. He wore a black T-shirt and black cargo pants with army boots.

Mr. Montgomery clapped his hands again. "Break off into pairs."

Trev turned toward me, a slow smile creeping up his handsome face. He wiggled his eyebrows, causing me to laugh, but before he could say anything, the commander was at my side, lightly grabbing my elbow.

"Why are you here?" he bluntly asked Trev.

Not one to be intimidated, Trev responded, "Because I can be. Do you have a reason that I shouldn't be?"

The commander looked like he wanted to tear Trev apart bit by bit. The atmosphere in the room changed as both guys stared at each other. Trev looked fierce, but the look on the commander's face had me wilting a little on the inside. There was no doubt about it; the man looked lethal.

The commander must've known they were drawing everyone's attention because he schooled his facial features as he turned toward me. "You came into the semester a little late." *Like two years late.* "I'd prefer you to work with someone who knows what they are doing."

Trev crossed his arms over his chest. "I know how to fight."

"Is that so?" The commander looked amused. "Nonetheless, Trevean, while you're under my roof, it's my rules. You will be working with Thomas." He pointed to a boy who was six feet tall and nothing but pure muscle. I couldn't help but wince.

Trev caught the look and laughed. "Don't you worry about me, beautiful. If I get any boo-boos, you'll have to doctor them for me."

I rolled my eyes while failing miserably to hide my smile. Trev was such a flirt.

Still not having released my elbow, the commander steered me away from Trev and to the edge of the mat. That damn humming thing started up again in full force.

"You'll be training with me today."

"You?" I scoffed. "Uh, why?"

"Most would be ecstatic to be training with me in hand-to-hand combat."

"I would think, by now, you've figured out that I'm not most."

"Yeah, I've witnessed that."

I begrudgingly followed him to the edge of the mat as I glanced around at all the kids who had begun to spar with one another. "So, you know Trev? But I thought he was a newbie just like me?"

"That's the way it looks, huh?"

"So, that's all I'm going to get from you? I mean,

obviously, there is some tension between the two of you."

"That's not for you to worry about. You need to worry about why one of your classes is hand-to-hand combat training and the next is weapon training." *Oh, good point.* "You missed out on two years. You are way behind."

"Tsk, tsk, Commander. My wand lit up a measly green, remember? Who could I possibly be training to fight?"

He flashed his green eyes to my face. "Listen—"

My traitorous heart tightened in my chest. Just the sound of his voice did funny things to me.

"—darken and demons won't care that you have little power. So, for your sake, I'm hoping that you're just a late bloomer."

"Oh, so you force me to a place where I'll be fighting those things? That's good thinking on your part. Bravo."

"You think that you were safe out there? Do you know what will happen when you turn eighteen? You will come into your powers, partially becoming a beacon to any demons nearby. And by the way, the plants that were moving behind me on testing day? That's abnormal. I will have to wager that your light will be pretty hard to hide. So, we train."

So, he had witnessed the plants dancing, and here I thought I had been super cool in hiding them from him.

I sat down on the mat facing him. My mind was racing while he was running me through stretching. I had dreams of kids fighting kids. Freaking kids!

"Will I only have to fight demons and darken?" I

wanted to see if he would be honest with me.

"Hopefully."

"You're not very forthcoming with info. Can you try not to be aloof for a minute?"

He clenched his jaw. "To give you an idea of what you're up against, both academies are after the same thing—something that could tip the balance. Your opponents will show you no mercy. You get to know your classmates, or you develop a close relationship with someone, none of that will matter if they choose to be on a different side, or if they choose to stay here and you decide to transfer to the Empowered Academy, so trust no one and try to be better than either person on either side of you."

WTH?

I looked around the room as everyone began to stretch. The students were laughing or talking with one another, and not one of them looked homicidal. Not like the kids I saw in my dreams.

What was the something to tip the balance that he referred to?

"When will you be able to answer my questions in full?"

"When you decide who you want to belong to."

I knew he meant which academy, but the way he said those words made heat swirl in my stomach. Holy angel babies. The man was smoking hot.

I tried to concentrate as he showed me a quick warm-up. He touched me just when absolutely necessary, but even that was enough to have me gnawing on my lip.

We went through the basic stances. At first, I was more than a little awkward, but once I loosened up, I found myself flowing from one position to the next like a lyrical dancer. I had always wanted to take dance lessons. I thought I would be good at it. Unfortunately, foster parents usually had their own kids to shuffle to afterschool sports. With schedules full, no one had been willing to add more to their plates. Guess this was a close second, if you just let your body glide and flow the way it needed to move.

"You're a natural," the commander said.

"Thanks." His compliment had me grinning.

"Now, let's learn basic blocks."

I concentrated hard on what he was saying. If I was honest with myself, maybe I was trying to impress him. Also, his warning rang so true that I became more than a little motivated. If I didn't escape this hell hole, then at some point, I would have to pick a side. There was no use in making friends when our paths might make us go in different directions. Then we would be looking at each other from across the battlefield.

I blocked another hit just to lose my concentration when I looked over to see how Trev was faring. He currently had the big guy pinned on the ground, a bead of sweat rolling down his face. Seeing where my gaze was, the commander swept out a foot and had me pinned almost in the exact position that Trev had his opponent pinned in.

Green eyes the color of the deepest sea hovered over me. His handsome face was contorted with anger. Everywhere his body touched me had my body humming with some unidentified need.

"Pay attention. I know there are things you don't understand yet, and you will eventually, but until then, do not lose focus. One day, these lessons could save your life."

I meant to sound outraged, but my voice came out husky. "Whoa. Easy on the rage, dude. There is no reason to be so intense."

"There is nothing about the academy that isn't intense. If you want to survive your first year, you must pay attention. And making gooey eyes at boys is not the way to stay alive." He sounded jealous.

My heart raced just at the thought that this man could be attracted to me. I forgot to breathe as his body hovered over mine, touching me just enough to have my mind spinning.

He glared at me. "You want to flirt? Then do it after school hours."

Whoops. Misread that one.

"Sure thing, boss."

He hopped off me with the agility of a cat. Meanwhile, I rolled onto all fours then slowly stood like I was geriatric.

After my embarrassing takedown, he set me up in front of a punching bag. He told me the drills that he wanted me to do while he made the rounds to different groups, critiquing everyone in the class.

Twenty minutes later, sweat dripped from me, and I was pretty sure I pulled something in my hamstring.

Just when I was about to beg for water, Mr. Montgomery

announced that it was time for us to go into our perspective locker rooms and get changed. Class was over. *Thank the heavens.*

The commander stopped me on the way to the locker room. "Since you've avoided the system for a while, most of the kids your age are way ahead of you. You're going to need extra practice."

"I can help her with that." A voice came over my shoulder.

I turned to see Trev looking annoyed with our commander. What was going on with these two?

The commander said, "Thanks, but I think she'll need the best." Turning his attention back to me, he said, "I'll send you the times I'm available to your dorm. Let me know what works best for you."

I stood there and watched the commander walk away.

Several girls made an attempt to stop him with questions on sparring. However, he politely excused himself each time.

Trev murmured something under his breath about privileged assholes.

"So," I said, "how do you know him?"

His eyes were still focused on the commander's back as he replied, "It's a boring conversation, and I don't want to waste any time on that sanctimonious asshole."

Okay, then. Now, I was dying to know. Maybe I could get Remy to help me figure out what the beef was between these two. I just knew it was going to be something epic.

My intuition was telling me that Trev was a good guy, but he was also hiding something.

We started walking toward the locker rooms. I didn't know what to say. Thanks again for this morning sounded weird, so I settled with, "I need to go change. I'll see you later."

Five minutes later, I had dried off from the quickest shower ever and was heading out of the locker rooms. I was a little disappointed that I didn't see Trev, who must've gone to his next class.

Out in the hall, a group of students was walking toward their next class. I noticed the blondes from earlier, Marlie-Beth and Angelina. As soon as they saw me, they started whispering like we were back in kindergarten. I hiked my backpack higher on my shoulder as I tried to make my way through the crowded hallway.

A leg jutted out in front of me, and I barely avoided tripping over it. I half-jumped, half-stumbled to the right to prevent face-planting on the marble floor.

A couple of kids snickered, and one kid was laughing like a hyena. I knew the laugh belonged to Marlie-Beth without looking.

I took deep breaths in and out, trying to calm my racing heart. Chills crawled down my spine as I felt Marlie-Beth's hatred slapping against me. When someone wanted to harm me, I could feel it. It had helped me a lot when I was little and bouncing around some foster homes that weren't too great. She didn't just want to embarrass the new kid.

She really wanted to cause me harm. Why someone would hate someone they barely knew was a mystery to me, but I knew I'd be stupid not to listen to my gut.

I started walking faster down the hall until I saw Trev leaning up against the wall. He smiled as he walked toward me.

"You okay?"

I nodded.

"Good. Let's go get some lunch."

"Listen, those girls hate me. You shouldn't associate with me. I think I need to eat by myself at lunch today."

He held the door open for me.

"Um. Were you listening?"

He nodded but continued to match me step for step.

"What in the world are you doing?"

"Um, it looks like I'm waiting on your unbelievably slow behind so I can walk you to lunch. Are you always this slow, or is it because you have little legs?"

"Hey!" I slapped him playfully on the arm. "I am of average height, thank you very much." I hefted my backpack up higher on my shoulder. "Seriously, though, maybe you shouldn't be seen talking with me."

"The only reason for me to stay away from you is if you got a freakishly large boyfriend named Tiny, then I might have to reconsider this friendship." He wiggled his eyebrows then tugged on my ponytail. "Never mind, it doesn't really matter because you might be worth getting pummeled for."

I sighed. "This is going to kill your image."

He tilted his head to the side and smiled, showing dimples. "You're saying, by walking the prettiest girl in this school to class, I will get negative reviews? I think I'll take my chances. After all, bad publicity is better than no publicity."

Well, this was just great. The new, unbelievably hot guy was showing me interest.

Getting a little frustrated that he didn't understand the importance of what I was trying to tell him, I said, "Here's the truth, buddy, I'm not here to make friends. In fact, I think that is the worst thing that I could possibly do."

A hand grazed my cheek. "The fear of betrayal, huh?"

"Yeah, something like that."

I could feel his eyes as I walked off. I liked Trev, but at the end of this journey, I'd rather not see his disgust if I chose a different side than him.

eight

I WAS SITTING UNDER A cherry blossom tree when a shadow appeared above me, having taken my lunch outside because it was a beautiful day and partly because I was trying to avoid Trev.

Gearing myself up for a fight, I gazed upward at the person who hovered over me. It was none other than the other newbie himself. I narrowed my eyes at him as he squatted down beside me on the grass.

"I'm not going to be able to shake you, am I?" I sighed.

He reached for the apple on my tray and took a big bite out of it. "You don't have the black plague. There is no reason we can't be friends. You don't even know which group you belong to or want to belong to. Try not to be so dramatic."

I looked over his shoulder to see Marlie-Beth and

Angelina staring at us from their outdoor lunch table and let out a loud groan. Man, I just couldn't seem to get off their radar today.

"Besides," he said, "it's not like you're going to escape your fate, let alone this place, so you'll need friends, and I'm putting in an application for the job."

I snatched my apple back from him. "Why are you so certain that I'm not going to escape?"

"That's an easy one. First, you are what you are. There is no amount of hiding that will change that. I don't know what your parents have or haven't told you, but I think you have a distorted image of what the academies are for. They can actually help you. Maybe you're just at the wrong academy. Why did you choose this one? Did your parents suggest it?"

"I missed the other testings, and I don't have parents."

A look of sympathy crossed his face, but I didn't want his pity.

"Do you really think that I'm safer here?"

He took my apple out of my hand and took another bite. "That's exactly what I'm saying. Out there, you are a loner; free game for either academy, which is okay, but that means you're free game for the demons, too. Demons don't mess with the Empowered Academy because they are under the safety of the darken, and demons won't mess with you here because they are afraid of the jerk who runs the place. My point is, academies are safer. Both places have free room and board, three meals a day, and behind either academy walls, you get a better understanding of who you are."

I looked him up and down. "Why do I have a feeling you already know who you are?"

He gave me a wink before he set my half-eaten apple back down on my tray. Then Trev glanced behind him to the large group surrounding Marlie-Beth and Angelina and laughed.

"What's so funny?"

"Those little witches over there are talking about you. Man, they are really jealous."

"I don't know why. And wait a second, you can hear them from here?"

"Yeah, it's part of my power." He looked away from the group. "I'm neither demi nor fully blessed. I'm actually a descendant from an angel. They call us Nephilim."

My mouth dropped open. I hadn't been expecting that.

He reached over and closed my jaw with a finger.

Nephilim? My mind was reeling. "You're not really here to enroll, are you?"

"No." I didn't think he was going to expand on his answer, but he finally said, "I'm Switzerland. I haven't chosen a side. Not because I'm undecided, but because I think this whole war is ridiculous. Do you know what I mean?"

I stared into his eyes for a long time. "I think I know exactly what you mean."

He elbowed me lightly. "And as far as you not

knowing why they'd be jealous, you are either fishing for compliments or are extremely naïve when it comes to the minds of catty girls." He took one look at my face and said, "Well, I can see that, unfortunately, it's the latter."

"So, fully blessed boy, how are you so familiar with the workings of catty girls?"

"I have sisters." He smirked.

I looked over at the group again, and that kid Devon was staring at me. "So, is Devon catty, too?"

"I hate to break it to you, cupcake, but saying he wants to tap that might be crude. But that's not hating on you. In fact, it's just the opposite, which probably just adds fuel to the fire when it comes to those felines who disguise themselves as girls."

I pushed my food around on my plate, contemplating what he was saying. Then I laid my fork down and looked across the courtyard to where the gardens faded into the woods. Was that the way that the Rocks, Dan and Dick, had brought me? If I could just find the way out, I would be free.

Trev followed my line of sight and sighed. "You really want out, don't you?"

I didn't say anything.

"You know what I think? I think you have more power than you're letting on. Why not embrace it?"

Because I was terrified that I'd be someone that people actually expected things from. I had always been a loner. Being part of a group or faction waging a war that I thought was beyond ridiculous wasn't me.

"I guess I'd rather be on a couch watching Netflix than swinging a sword."

He laughed. "Well, then it's up to me to change your mind." He stood up. "I'm going to go check out the school gym. Are you going to be okay out here by yourself?"

I rolled my eyes. "Seriously? Of course I am."

"Hey, as far as anyone knows, I'm just an average blessed kid enrolled at the school."

I gave him a nod to let him know I understood.

He kissed the top of my head. "See you soon, beautiful."

I watched him walk across the courtyard. Every girl along the way tried to catch his eye. The boy really was nice to look at.

I pulled up some grass and started braiding the small pieces together, thinking about what I was going to do, when I felt that familiar humming in my chest. I jerked my head up to see the commander walking out of the cafeteria. He was with a shorter man who was very animated as he talked. The commander kept nodding while they walked on the sidewalk toward the outdoor weapons training facility where I had my next class.

I couldn't help watching him walk away. The man was absolutely stunning. Raw power strummed off him. I wondered what his story was. How long had he been here? What was his age when he had graduated?

He must've felt my eyes on him, because he stopped and slowly started turning my way. The distance between us was at least a football field, but when his eyes locked on to mine, it felt like he was mere inches away. I should have averted my eyes, but God help me, I couldn't. There was something about him that was so familiar.

He had stopped walking, his attention fully on me. The shorter man didn't seem to notice that he no longer had a listening audience.

The most beautiful smile I had ever seen ignited on his handsome face. Then he raised one of his eyebrows in question. I narrowed mine in answer.

I finally had the courage to break eye contact and slowly stood while I gathered my things. I didn't look at him again, but I could tell he was still where I had last seen him, because my body still had that familiar warmth.

I took out a folded piece of paper from my back pocket and studied the schedule. My classes ranged from learning about archangels to hand-to-hand combat, weapon training, cardio—I guessed to be able to physically run from future enemies, whomever they might be—magic, and moral philosophy.

I glanced over to Marlie-Beth's table before I headed across campus. I could feel the evil radiating from her. She had to be a demi touched by a darken. But what about me? Did I have dark powers swirling inside me? I shuddered at the thought.

Forget who I was going to become. Who did I *want* to be? Now that was a great question.

nine

WHEN A KNOCK SOUNDED ON my door, I quickly got up to answer it, considering Remy was still passed out. I had six classes today, and all Remy had done was sleep.

I swung open the door, finding a skinny brunette standing there. She shifted a suitcase in her hands as she nervously smiled at me.

"Yes?" I asked.

"Um. Hi. I think we're supposed to be roommates."

I looked behind me to see Remy sitting up.

"WTF did she just say?"

I looked at the girl. "Sorry, I already have a roommate."

She pointed to a piece of paper. "But it says here that—"

"Sorry," I said, shrugging. "Must be some kind of mistake."

There was no reason to further explain, so I gently shut

the door in her face.

Remy threw her hands up in the air. "Un-freaking-believable. People treat me as if I just don't exist."

I laughed as she lay back on the bed with all the dramatics of a first-rate queen.

Fifteen minutes later, another knock sounded on the door. This one was more forceful.

"Don't worry, Remy; I've got it." I quipped when she didn't move.

Feeling that now familiar heat rise in my chest, I knew who would be on the other side before I swung open the door.

I opened the door to see the commander glaring down at me, taking his sweet time as he raked his green eyes over my body before he cleared his throat.

"Um, hi?" I said.

"I thought that Rachel would be a good fit for you. She's kind, and she could actually use a friend. Not to mention the fact that she's already showing great potential. She is fully blessed, and her power level is high, and you could use a good ally." I shook my head, causing him to narrow his eyes in annoyance. "Every student here must have a roommate. You don't have the authority to pick and choose who you room with."

"Cool, but I already have a roommate." Geez, this was about to get awkward.

He pushed past me and into my room. He made a gesture to the unmade bed. "Yeah, I can see that."

Remy stood up and circled the commander. "Oh, my gawd. He is so freaking yummy. And what is that smell? It's like spicy sex on a stick."

I smiled, causing the commander to frown. "This isn't funny."

"No, of course not," I said.

Remy pinned her black hair back with a hand so she could get closer to the commander, causing the man to brace himself. He scanned the room, as if he knew something wasn't quite right in the air. Then he ran a hand down the back of his neck as Remy got even closer to him.

Remy bent at the waist. "Have you seen his ass? It's perfect. Do me an itsy-bitsy favor and ask him if he goes commando."

"Yeah, I'm not doing it."

Confusion colored the commander's face. "Doing what?" Then he tensed up, and my eyes involuntarily went to his coiled muscles. The guy was stacked. His masculinity was almost overwhelming. "Gabriella, who is your roommate?"

"Hmm?" I jerked my eyes away from his biceps. "Oh, I thought you'd never ask. Remy."

"Remy Rodriguez?"

I looked over at Remy, who said, "Let thy name roll off those divine lips. Say it again, sugar."

I tried to cover my laugh with an unsuccessful cough. "Yes."

The commander looked around the room. "Interesting.

I knew you'd be powerful."

I shrugged. "Don't know what you're talking about."

"Sure you don't." He studied me. "So, you have death in you, and you're demonstrating those powers with Remy."

"Well, that's a creepy way to put it."

"You know what I meant. How long have you been able to see the dead?"

My eyes dropped to his muscular chest. "Since I was five. I thought it was normal until my foster parents returned me to DSS. When you claim to see apparitions, you get rehomed."

He swallowed thickly, his Adam's apple moving. Something unreadable crossed over his eyes before he took a step back. Then he dipped his head for a moment before he took another look around my room. "I'll tell Rachel that I was wrong and that you do, in fact, already have a roommate. Tell Remy I'm sorry about what happened to her. She was a good student." He was the only person who was solemn in this room.

I looked over at Remy, who was still staring at the commander's butt.

"Ask him," Remy said, "or I swear I'll make your granny panties levitate out of your drawer and into the hall. That's going to be freaking embarrassing for you."

I blurted. "Do you wear underwear?"

The commander looked startled as he pulled back from me a bit. "You want to know if I wear underwear?"

My cheeks were on fire as I nodded. I darted my eyes to

Remy then back to him. He tracked my motions, and a look of understanding crossed his face.

"No. No, I do not."

Remy pumped a fist into the air. "Knew it! Gabriella, seriously, you need to throw yourself at this fine specimen. He is gorg!"

The commander looked at me, staring off into space beside him, and he cleared his throat. "Things are getting a little weird, so I'm going to head out. See you at orientation."

"Yeah, see ya."

As soon as he left, I threw a pillow at Remy. Of course it went right through her and hit the wall, but she still knew my intent. "Dude, that was uncomfortable as hell."

"Seriously doubt that," Remy said. "I hear that hell is extremely uncomfortable. Still not paying attention in archology class?"

I rolled my eyes at my friend. "So, the commander said he was sorry about what happened to you. Do you want to talk about it?"

"Oh, I wish, but I don't remember. It is said that if you die tragically and it's too much for you to handle, you forget the way you bit the dust. It must've been gory AF, because I don't recall a damn thing. Then again, I cry watching *All Dogs Go to Heaven*, so it could be that I'm just easily traumatized."

I nodded like that made sense. "Do you want me to ask him for you? I mean, it sounded like he knew."

She shook her head. "No, not right now. Maybe later. I just get down and out when I think about that night, and there is nothing worse than a gloomy-ass bitch that's a ghost."

"Okay, change of subject, it is. I really want to know what the beef is between the commander and Trev. My gut is telling me it's something huge, and if I just ask, they aren't going to tell me."

"I can totally help with that. Let me see what I can dig up."

"Seriously? You don't mind?"

"What the hell else am I going to do? I'm officially the resident ghost P.I. on the case. I just wish I had a fanny pack and a recorder."

I laughed.

"What? Fanny packs are so making a comeback." She floated toward the door. "Why don't you get some rest? Tomorrow, after your classes, is the big revealing day. It's exhausting. You go to bed, and I'm going to go out and hunt for clues and also haunt some bitches. Any suggestions?"

"Marlie-Beth and Angelina," I said without hesitation. "They are nas-ty."

She clapped her hands. "I'll make them cry. Teach them not to mess with my girl."

I laughed as she went right through our door, not bothering to open it.

Remy was the first ghost that I truly appreciated visiting

me. I guessed it was because the other ghosts that had popped in from time to time always got me in trouble. By the time I had figured out to keep my mouth shut, I had already been labeled as a troubled child. Not that I was listing the pros to this place, but if I were, not being judged because I saw ghosts was definitely a positive.

I brushed my teeth and crawled into bed, hoping that I didn't have another dream. Unfortunately, I wasn't so lucky.

ten

ABBADONA ADDRESSED THE GROUP OF *fifteen archangels. "I am disappointed in all of you."*

The archangels bowed their heads in shame while Camaella stood slightly to the right of the group with a smirk on her face, while Abbadona battled to control his anger.

"None of you truly understand the ramifications of what you've done." The mighty angel paced in front of the lot. *"You all assumed that all the humans would die, and not only was that not the case, but more importantly, you were told not to interfere, and yet all of you did. Whose idea was this?"*

Sandalphon could tell that Gabriel, who was the most selfless of all of them, was about to confess. She would gladly take the fall for her brothers and sisters, and he couldn't allow that, so he quickly spoke. "Abbadona, it was my idea."

Uriel nodded, along with Michael.

"Yes, it was our idea, as well," Michael said.

Uriel said, "The three of us, actually."

Abbadona looked at the three warriors with a mixture of pride and anger. "Do not lie to me." he boomed, causing Ariel to weep. "Love for humanity got you into this mess, and love for your brothers and sisters is causing you to further sin by lying to me. Sometimes love in itself is a sin."

Ariel wept harder. She felt as if it was all her fault.

Gabriel grabbed her sister's hand. "Shh. It's okay, love."

Camaella, who had been standing to the side, snickered at Ariel's distress.

Abbadona turned on his heel, narrowing his eyes at the beautiful redhead. "You take true enjoyment from their pain." He walked over to her, causing Camaella to stand up tall. When he laid a hand on her arm, her eyes widened. "I could feel the evil in you. You no longer possess angel-like qualities. You lack forgiveness, warmth, and virtue."

She glared at the fifteen angels behind Abbadona.

He shook his head. "Always so quick to blame everyone else when it is you who is in the wrong. Only you can be held accountable for your own actions."

He took a step back from her. "Here is what is to be done with the fifteen of you. You are to be cast from heaven. All of you will be permanent defenders of earth."

Jophiel gasped. "We will be fallen angels?"

Abbadona shrugged. "You should have thought about the consequences of your actions before this moment. You will always bear the mark of the fallen. There is nothing I can do about that, but that does not need to be your title." He jerked his thumb toward Camaella. "And this one has opened the gates of hell with her treachery. The fifteen of you tried to save as many as you could, and now the humans will need constant protection just to survive."

Chamuel asked, "Exactly what did Camaella do?"

Abbadona started to glow brighter, showing how upset he truly was. "Why, she alerted the original fallen to the archangels' plan. Some of the ones you touched and blessed, they have tracked down."

"They are not dead," Ariel said. "If they were, we'd feel it."

"No, not dead, but forever altered."

Without warning, the angels fell, their screams piercing the night.

In order to get to earth, they had to endure hell first, and their once white wings transformed from a brilliant, pure white to pitch black.

I tossed in my sleep, feeling their pain as if it were my own. I clenched the sheets as they continued to fall, their grief consuming me. Finally, I woke up with tears streaming down my face.

Sitting up in bed, I wondered how the archangels fared on earth and what had been Camaella's punishment.

I used the top sheet of my bed to wipe my face. I had dreams of the angels before, but they were fuzzy and sporadic. Why was I having such vivid dreams of the fifteen archangels and Camaella now? Was it because I was in the academy?

I knew I wouldn't find the answers tonight, just as I knew that sleeping was no longer an option.

eleven

"STUDENTS, WE ARE GOING TO be working with partners today. Unfortunately, there is an odd number of students. For the ones of you who don't seem to pay attention in my class," Mrs. Fields said, looking pointedly at me before continuing, "let me explain to you why an odd number would be a problem. One of you will be without a partner." Smiling at me, she said, "All right, students, pick your partners."

Well, that settled it. The woman definitely had it out for me. She knew I would be the odd man out, and she was prematurely relishing in my soon-to-be embarrassment.

Remy sat on the corner of my desk. "What a grade-A bitch." She stood up and walked to her desk. "That's it, I'm going to mess with her OCD."

My eyes widened as papers began to fly, Post-Its were

crumpled over, and her computer went crashing to the ground.

Mrs. Fields looked around in horror as the students started whispering.

Remy jumped up on her desk and started disco dancing while ironically singing "Staying Alive." It took everything I had not to laugh. I was biting the inside of my cheek so hard I tasted blood.

Mrs. Fields pushed the button on the intercom, calling for Mr. Habb. How the moral philosophy teacher would be helpful was beyond me.

Remy shrieked, "Eek! That's the po-po for ghosts. She's on to me. Gotta run, babe." She flew through the wall to the outside of the school while Mrs. Fields continued to turn in a circle.

When nothing happened for a few minutes, Mrs. Fields began to straighten up her desk with shaky hands. "Don't think that a ghost will get you out of your work." Her voice caught, and her eyes continually shifted all around the room. Obviously, ghosts were her Achilles' heel.

"Pair up, students, and get to work."

There was a ton of grumbles, but everyone started moving their chairs.

I dropped my head and concentrated on the assigned twenty-one questions before me. We were to identify the fifteen archangels by the descriptions of their personalities. I would be without a partner, so it'd take me twice as long. Might as well go ahead and get started.

There was a loud grunt as a desk screeched on the floor as it scooted closer to mine.

"What are these desks made of?"

I looked up in time to see a scrawny kid who had to be six feet tall plopping down in her seat that was now freakishly close to mine. She pushed back her mop of curls before she propped her chin on her hands and began to stare at me.

Um ... "What are you doing?"

She stacked her workbook and papers on her desk, making her unruly, bright orange hair fall in her face. Pushing it back into place, she said, "You needed a partner, and I needed a partner, so ..." She trailed off.

I smiled. "So, you thought you would throw in your lot with mine?"

"Something like that. I'm Hannah, by the way. My parents took one look at my hair and named me after Archangel Haniel." Her orange curls bounced as she moved in her seat. Her blue eyes were bright in her pale face. "So, Mrs. Fields? Can we talk about how she was purposefully trying to embarrass you? Which makes me wonder why. I mean, she doesn't really like anyone, but she *loathes* you. I cannot stand her, and since she can't stand you ..." She gave a little shrug. "Jokes on her, though. Look over my shoulder and see what we've done."

Three girls were arguing with who should be partners.

"One of us was bound to be the odd man out. Kids think I'm eccentric because, let's face it, weird is too harsh a word, and I deserve better, and you're a newbie, so everyone will shy away from you at first. At least until after orientation."

I raised an eyebrow. "Why is that?"

"There are two categories that you can fall into. The fully blessed or a demi, and then there are sub-categories in each of those two. We all get rated. If your blessing is minimal, people will ignore you. If you're a high-level demi or a powerful fully blessed, you are automatically part of the *cool crowd*. Everyone loves a warrior." She rolled her eyes while making a gagging motion with her index finger stuck in her mouth.

"So, I'll find out all that at orientation?"

"Basically."

"So, what are you?"

"Fully blessed. A darken got his hands on me last year." The girl looked embarrassed for a brief second. "I'm only seventeen. I don't think anyone under eighteen has their powers yet, at least not that I'm aware of, but I still know what I'm capable of. They told me my level of power will be a two. So, when my powers do come to me, I won't be awe-inspiring. Half the damn demis in this place are already more powerful than I'll ever become."

Interesting. I had dogs talking to me, trees trying to grope me, and I was actively communicating with my dead roomie. What did that mean?

"So, we find out what power level we are at the ceremony?"
"Yeah."

Mr. Habb had finally arrived and was talking with Mrs. Fields about the possible ghost, though she did manage to stop mid-conversation to shoot us a glare. "You ladies better be working on the assignment that I gave you and nothing else."

I made a great show of reading the worksheet in front of me while, out of the side of my mouth, I said, "We better work."

"Yep, I can feel her eyes on us." She snickered. "Man, she hates you."

I scribbled down an answer. "How do you know it's not you?"

"She would have to notice me to not like me, and I personally think that would be a step up from being invisible." She pointed to the first question that I had answered on my paper. "That one is wrong."

Huh?

"Which angel is always calm and sympathetic and forgiving? The answer is Zadkiel."

I sighed as I erased my answer. How would knowing the angels' personalities help me in real life? And shouldn't all angels be calm, sympathetic, and forgiving?

Hannah chuckled as I aggressively wrote the correct answer. "You'll learn it eventually."

"And if I don't?"

"Then you won't pass the class." She was quickly filling out her worksheet. "Your first day here was crazy, huh? I was out in the hall when Marlie-Beth and Angelina were being their natural sweet selves."

Putting my long hair in a ponytail to give my hands something to do, I said, "Yeah, well, I think everyone probably saw that confrontation."

"You know what I also witnessed? That newbie that is so freaking hot come to your rescue. So, are you two an item now?"

I laughed. "No. Trev is just my friend, even though I tried to convince him that, by being my friend, it'll make it harder in the long run. You know, when we have to decide which academy we will be staying at."

"Well, don't worry about warning me. I'm pretty sure that I'm getting kicked out at the end of the year. My powers are too low."

"You want to stay here?"

"I do. There is a few here at the academy who are horrible, but for the most part, we're like a little family. Besides, the commander is fair and also the hottest male I've ever seen in my life."

We both laughed, causing Mrs. Fields to come over to our desks.

"Is there something funny about the archangels?"

"No, ma'am," I said, shaking my head.

For the rest of the period, we didn't talk.

After Hannah did her work, she switched her paper with mine so I could have her answers. I gave her a fist bump before I looked down at the correct answers and began to copy.

Why was it so important to learn about the angels in my dreams? What did they have to do with the academy? Other than, at some point, they touched humans and made demis. Why did I have powers before I was eighteen? The questions just kept adding up. Nothing made sense, and my fear of the unknown grew every minute I was in this place.

Dread curled around me like a fist.

twelve

THE REST OF THE DAY flew by. Hand-to-hand combat was fun, and without the commander showing up, I was allowed to partner with Trev. He wasn't lying when he said that he was an amazing fighter. He was almost as good as the commander. However, he wasn't as intense and was gentler in the way he sparred with me.

Trev came up behind me. "You need to learn how to get out of a chokehold." He pressed his body against mine, and my stomach fluttered. "When you feel my hand come across your chest, I want you to immediately drop your chin."

I did as he asked, lowering my chin, just as his other hand came up to clasp his hand that was under my neck.

"Good. Now give a step to the side as you grab my wrist. I want your left hand to shoot down to the groin but don't actually hit the jewels, beautiful."

I gave a nervous laugh as I moved slowly. "Now what?"

"Now, you've made me double over. You're going to take that same arm and drive your elbow into my nose."

We repeated the steps over and over until I was moving a little quicker. Mr. Montgomery stopped by and praised us before he moved on to the next group. By the time the bell rang, I felt confident I could get out of a chokehold.

When lunch time came around, Hannah and Trev sat with me at a picnic table outside. Remy was there, too, trying to guess if Trev went commando, but I didn't tell anyone that. I was making friends, so I didn't want to weird them out right away. I would wait to tell them that I could see the dead.

The rest of the day flew by pretty fast. My weapons training class wasn't going great, but I hadn't hurt myself yet, so that was a positive. We were all still in the process of trying out different types of weapons. The bow wasn't my friend yet, but I had hopes I'd get better.

I was totally slaying cardio training; up to running three miles, which was amazing, in my opinion, considering I had never run a mile before the academy.

After training, I did a quick lay of the land to see that, unfortunately, the whole academy had wards surrounding it to keep other beings out and to keep us in. If I had to escape this place, it was going to be tricky. In the meantime, I would learn everything I could about the people in charge of the academy, including the commander himself. Knowing the academy leaders better would help me to avoid them if I had to escape. I had asked Remy earlier if the commander had a way of tracking someone if they left the academy, but she was no help. She laughed for a solid five minutes.

I tabled my future worries for the time being and had just gotten out of the shower. I was trying to decide what to wear for orientation tonight. My choices were slim—something out of my duffel bag or a school uniform. Every outfit I owned had been given to me and was secondhand. Most had tears or holes, and every piece I laid out on the bed, Remy winced at. It looked like I would be wearing pleather and a T-shirt.

I grabbed a uniform and was about to head to the bathroom when Remy pretended to faint.

"What?" I said. "This is all I have?"

Remy daintily scooped her hair over to one side. "Baby, that's the saddest thing I've ever heard. I'm currently more depressed now than when I found out I was dead. You can't wear that. Everyone will be dressed up in their finest."

But this was my finest.

I sighed as I plopped down on my bed.

Remy stood up and gave me air kisses. "Listen to your bestie. Go, do your hair and makeup. Let me worry about the clothing."

I sighed but did as she asked.

Thirty minutes before the orientation started, there was a hard knock on my door. I answered it, still wearing my robe, even though I knew who was on the other side.

The commander stood there briefly in shock before he closed his mouth. "Um, may I come in?"

"Sure, why not?"

He carried a black garment bag in his hands that gently laid across my bed before turning to me. "I had an unexpected visitor today. I believe it was your friend Remy."

"Why do you say that?"

"Someone broke into my personal quarters and wrote in pink lipstick on the mirror."

"What did it say?"

He grimaced. "It started out with something inappropriate about my physique and ended with an idle threat."

I smiled. My ghost was one of a kind. She could hit on you, and then make a threat and literally give zero shits. I loved her.

I looked at the garment bag. "So, you were forced to come up with something?"

The commander shrugged. "Actually, I'm embarrassed that I didn't think of it sooner. Most kids are ecstatic to come to the academy. Their parents send them off with cookies and a credit card. You wouldn't believe the shipments Richard has to pick up every week."

I held my hands out to the sides. "Sorry, no parents or credit cards."

"Yeah, I know. That's why I should've thought of it sooner."

Great, he pitied me for my sad life.

I unzipped the bag, revealing a fiery red dress with a back that laced up like a corset. I ran my hand over the beads. "It's beautiful." And according to the tag, it would fit me. "How did you know my size?"

His green eyes were molded to my body, reminding me that I stood there in just a robe. "Lucky guess."

"How did you get it so fast?"

He sported a cocky grin. "I have wings."

My eyes bulged. "When will I get mine?"

He laughed. "Only the fully blessed get wings, and it's after your birthday." His brows came together. "Well, usually, but nothing about you is textbook." I watched his eyes travel to my naked legs again. He cleared his throat. "I'll let you get dressed."

As he walked toward the door, I picked up the bottom of the dress, feeling the material between my hands. I had never had anything so fancy.

Before he closed the door behind him, I said, "Thank you for this."

He gave me a nod. "My pleasure."

The way he said that word had heat surging through me.

He briefly narrowed his eyes on my lips before he quickly left, taking all the oxygen in the room with him. I didn't understand my reaction to him, but I had to admit that there was a deep attraction that I couldn't explain.

Twenty-five minutes later, I was wearing the red gown that fit me like a glove on top before slightly flaring out at the hips. The dress shimmered in the light of the gymnasium where the orientation would be held as my heels clicked on the floor.

Taking in my surroundings, I saw a raised platform at the back of the gym, with chairs placed in a semi-circle so that everyone could face the stage, a path through the middle.

I ran a hand down the nicest thing I'd ever owned once again, thankful that Remy and the commander had come up with something for me to wear since everyone I passed was in evening attire.

The gymnasium was crowded, so I skirted to the edges in search of finding my friend, Hannah, which wasn't hard, considering she was as tall as a skyscraper, and her orange hair was like a torch—visible from a mile away.

Before I could make my way over to her, I felt a hand lightly touch my elbow. Coming out of the shadows was the commander.

He gave me an appraising look before his lips slightly tilted up. "You're not thinking of running, are you?"

"No, just thought it would be easier to go around the

mass of bodies." His hand was still on my arm, and I did my best to act unaffected.

He took me in slowly from my head to my toes, making the familiar heat in my belly rise like a tidal wave. "You look stunning."

The salvia dried in my mouth.

"I'll let you get to your friends, but just remember that tonight is just determining a piece of who you are." He let go of my arm, and then I watched as he cut through the middle of the crowd without any issue. They just naturally parted for him, as if everyone knew they should get out of the way without qualm for something so magnificent. I didn't blame them. Power seemed to radiate from him with every stride he took.

I caught sight of Hannah again and made my way over to her.

Her mouth dropped open when she saw me. "Wow. Looking good, friend."

"Thanks."

Trev came up behind me, sending tingles down my spine as he whispered in my ear, "Hey, beautiful."

"Hey," I said way more huskily than I intended. It should be illegal to have this many gorgeous men under one roof.

Remy floated over to our group. "Damn, girl. The commando commander did good. Are you wearing a bra?"

"What is it with you and undergarments?"

Trev stepped to the side as his eyebrows drew together.

"Um ... Are you talking to me? 'Cause, if so, this conversation is heading in a great direction."

Remy started dying with laughter.

I waved a hand. "No, no. Just talking to myself. They say you do that when stressed, and these heels have ramped up my anxiety. I don't know if I'm going to wobble or fall. Should we go sit?"

Hannah said, "Newbies have to sit in the front row, but I'll catch up with you afterward."

Trev bowed at me before he extended his elbow. "Shall I escort you?"

I laughed at his theatrics. "Why, of course, kind sir."

We took the first couple of chairs that we came to, and as soon as we sat down, the gym lights dimmed. My knee bounced up and down as I let my nerves get the best of me. I didn't know what to expect, but I had a feeling that, after tonight, my life was going to be changed. I had learned a long time ago to trust my gut.

An older woman came out onto the stage and sat in one of the two chairs on the platform. Her gray hair was beautifully braided over one shoulder. Then the commander walked to the center of the platform, and immediately everyone in the audience quietened.

"We recently found four more blessed students," he addressed all the students at the academy. "Today, we will officially welcome them. If they are demis, we will find out what line they come from, along with their power level. If they are fully blessed, we will announce them as so." His eyes landed on me briefly before he continued, "The first one on our list is Angie McBeth."

Angie, a girl with long legs and short blonde hair, hopped up onto the stage in excitement. She sat in the vacant chair, as the older woman shuffled a deck.

Trev leaned in close to me, his hot breath tickling my ear. "The old woman already knows what we're capable of. She is just doing all this for show."

I turned to him. "You think so?"

"Yeah, the commander gets off with the whole hoopla of everything."

I faced forward again to find the commander's face set in stone. He didn't need words. The way he was glaring at Trev, it was apparent that, if Trev gave him an excuse for an ass-whooping, the commander would jump on it.

"I think he heard you," I murmured.

"Maybe. Or maybe it's because"—he leaned in really close this time, his bottom lip touching my earlobe—"I'm the one sitting next to you."

I looked back at the commander. Now he was focused on the girl on stage, but his body language was still taut. His jaw was clenched so hard that it was a wonder he didn't break his teeth.

Whatever was going on between the commander and Trev, I didn't want to be a part of it. One, it wasn't my fight; and two, I might have to make a run for it soon. Plus, I didn't want to witness Trev getting his ass served to him. Trev was, without a shadow of a doubt, the best in class in weapons training and hand-to-hand combat. He could beat all the students without trying, but I had a feeling he wasn't anywhere close to beating the man on stage.

I focused on the old lady as she turned over a card. She then reached for the girl's hands. Within seconds, the older woman was smiling as she held up a card with an empress on it. Then she held up one finger for the commander.

The commander said, "Congratulations, Angie, you're a demi. You come from Michael's line, with a category one healing."

The kid who sat on the other side of me mumbled, "That's weak. If you get hurt, a first-aid kit will probably help you better than her."

His friend in the second row of seats shushed him. "It could be worse. At least they are letting her stay."

I looked over at Trev to see if he heard them. He gave me a wink. "You're going to be fine."

I whispered, "Why are you sitting here with us if you're wanting to remain neutral?"

He whispered back, "I like ruffling the commander's feathers."

I didn't pay attention as the kid who sat next to me was called up. I really wanted to know the history between Trev and the commander.

The lady shuffled the cards, and my mind drifted. Maybe if I was a one, they would kick me out of the academy. Wouldn't that be nice? I mean, what could a level one bring to the table? I would learn to be a master at bottling up my powers. I had passed a darken wearing the Empowered Academy uniform once before on the street and they hadn't noticed anything extraordinary about me.

My eyes landed on the commander. I had a feeling that he didn't intend on calling Trev up. Earlier, he had said there were four new blessed, yet there were five of us sitting in the row. I was pretty sure that was why Trev jumped up and headed toward the stage before the next student could be called.

He had so much swagger as he walked up the side steps to the stage. He didn't greet the commander like the others; instead, he smirked. The commander never showed any kind of emotion as Trev walked in front of him. They definitely hated one another. Maybe it was an alpha male thing? I just hoped Trev didn't take it too far with his cockiness.

I laughed as Trev sat down in the adjacent seat and gave the older woman a smile as she shuffled the cards. When she didn't react, he added a wink, causing me to laugh. His flirting had no boundaries. After a few seconds, the older woman smiled at Trev before she winked back. The charmer was getting charmed. She pointed to the card on the far left.

The commander said, "What a surprise. It looks like you are Nephilim. Born from one of the original fallen and have been touched by Michael."

Trev stood and did a mock bow. "Everyone's favorite bodyguard," he said, and then he gave me an encouraging nod.

The kids behind me gasped, breaking my eye contact with Trev. I looked over to see the older lady holding up a number five for a power level.

Trev crossed his arms over his chest as he smirked at the commander, who didn't look at all impressed as he announced that Trev could find his seat.

Almost all the kids were clapping and cheering as Trev exited off the stage.

The commander wasn't shocked that Trev was Nephilim or a level five. What was I missing?

The kid next to me almost squealed when he said, "Can you believe that? An actual Nephilim. That's crazy."

Everyone was whispering with excitement as if Trev was a celebrity.

He sat down next to me and squeezed my knee. "Looks like you're up, beautiful."

Just then, the commander called my name.

This was mortifying, having to go up on stage in front of so many people. I kept my head down as I passed the commander and found my way to the seat. My hands shook as the elderly woman shuffled the cards, and then she reshuffled. It was like she could feel my anxiety from where she was and wanted to drag this out. She flipped over a card, and then another. She kept flipping until the whole damn deck was facing up. Then her hand shook as she reached for mine. She closed her eyes briefly, and then just stared at me.

After fifteen seconds that felt more like an hour, I looked

over to the commander, whose brows were crinkled together. The crowd started to whisper, but not with excitement like how they had with Trev. *Oh no.* Whatever was happening wasn't good.

The commander walked over to us and squatted in front of the older lady. "What is it, Sariel?"

She shook her head. "More than one archangel has laid their hands on her. She is part of the prophecy."

That didn't sound good

"What level am I?" *Please say one, please say one.*

"You don't have a level."

I let out a breath of relief.

"There is no way to rate what you are."

Well, shit.

I looked at the commander. "Maybe it's a mistake?"

He didn't answer me. What's worse? He didn't look shocked by Sariel's announcement. Instead, he whispered back to Sariel, "Has she been touched by a darken?"

She shook her head then told him, "We've taken too long. They will know something is up. Announce her as a demi, but give her a middle of the road power."

"Why would she lie?" I asked.

"To protect you," the commander said as he stood up.

He faced the group of students. "Students, it looks as if we have another demi, but we are unsure of which line she comes from. Sariel has narrowed it down to two."

The crowd erupted into whispers and murmurs.

Sariel pointed to the card of Gabriel, the beautiful angel

with long, brown hair and a warm smile. Her card read, "*Judgment.*" Then Sariel pointed to the card of Azrael, formidable warrior who stood proud. The bottom of his card read, "*Death.*" When Sariel then held up three fingers, the commander congratulated me in front of the audience.

I stood numbly from my chair and made my way back down to my seat. No one cheered for me the way they had done Trev.

The old lady said I had been blessed by more than one angel. How was that even possible?

I sat down in my chair, ignoring the murmurs around me. I wasn't sure if the kids were buying that dear old Sariel was confused by whom I'd been touched by. Sweat was dripping down my back.

Did she say prophecy? *Oh, hell no.* I needed out of this school, like yesterday. I didn't know precisely what all this meant for me, but I knew it wasn't good. I *had* to escape.

Immediately after the commander dismissed us, we all went toward the dining hall, where there were long tables shoved together with food laid upon them buffet style. I went through the motions of preparing a plate, even though the thought of eating right at this moment made my stomach queasy.

Hannah snagged us an empty table, and I shuffled toward it in a daze. Trev sat down on my right and Hannah on my left. Remy gave me some kind of hand gesture to let me know she'd be back later. One could only hope she was going off to wreak havoc on "the crew."

Hannah peppered Trev with questions. "So, how do you feel about being a Nephilim?"

He gave her a shrug. "I don't feel any different."

Hannah blushed before turning to me. "And you! The mighty oracle is confused over your lineage. What was all that about?"

I shrugged. "I guess, because my powers haven't fully manifested yet, it's hard to decipher."

"That is what the commander would like us to believe," Trev scoffed. "I'd like to point out that a lot of students' powers haven't manifested yet, but they still know what angel has touched them."

I stopped pushing the food around on my plate. "I'm just as confused as you guys."

He narrowed his eyes on me before he gave me a smile. "You're right. I'm sorry. I really just don't trust the commander."

"Why's that?"

Trev tapped his fingers on the table as he looked in the distance. I wasn't sure if he had heard me. "Not all is as it seems here. Look at all these kids."

We all took our time looking around the cafeteria. Everyone was in their own little groups, laughing and talking. A band was starting up, and kids were heading toward the dance floor.

"What exactly are we supposed to be looking at?" I asked.

"They are all so happy to be here. They think that they are blessed to have some amount of angel in them. They have no clue. We're all just pawns."

I shared a look with Hannah. She appeared just as confused as I was. I knew from my dreams that this place wasn't what it was cracked up to be, but what exactly did Trev know and how did he know it?

"What are you trying to say?"

He ran a tired hand over his face. "Forget it." He pushed back from the table and held a hand out to me. "Will you dance with me?"

"Um ..."

His eyes twinkled. "Come on; you're all dolled up, music is playing. Dance with me."

I put my hand in his, and Hannah wiggled her eyebrows at me, making me laugh. I followed him through the crowd and out onto the dance floor where he wrapped his arms around me and pulled me in close as the fast beat slowed into a sweet melancholy. For a minute, neither one of us said anything.

Finally, he broke the silence. "You always look beautiful, but tonight, you look ravishing."

I dipped my head to hide the blush. "Thank you."

"You know you can tell me anything, right?"

I nodded. "Yeah, you, too. Like what's the story between you and the commander and what is the reason that you are really here."

He sighed. "No, I refuse to ruin the night."

After the song ended, he asked, "Would you like some punch?"

"Sure."

As I watched him walk through the crowd, my heart thrummed and I knew who had come up behind me.

Without looking, I said, "Hello, Commander."

"You want to dance?"

That had my head swiveling. I took in his massive chest with a tattoo peeking out of the tuxedo collar. Then I let my eyes slowly travel up to his face. He rewarded me with a knowing smirk.

My insides clenched with desire. No one should be allowed to be that hot. It was a sin. And there was no way that I could press up against him and keep my wits or be able to walk away without looking like a simpering fool.

"Nope, I think I'm good."

His smile grew. "I can promise I dance better than him, too."

I rolled my eyes. "Must everything be a competition?"

"Only when the prize is worthy."

"Isn't there some kind of rules against teachers asking students to dance?"

His eyes were twinkling. I was pretty sure he was trying not to laugh. "If I wasn't immortal, technically, we would be almost the same age. Also, we're fighting a war against the demons and the darken. Life can be short; why not enjoy every moment while you can?"

He had a point. One that I chose to ignore. "Are you planning on telling me how it is possible that I have been touched by more than one angel?"

He grimaced. "It's complicated. I'll try to explain as much as I can. Tomorrow, though. Tonight, we celebrate.

"Well, in that case, I need air."

He grabbed my elbow before I could retreat. "Tell me, do you have dreams?"

When I was younger, I had my first dream of the academy. I remembered it vividly because it was a nightmare. There were teenagers killing teenagers to make sure they didn't become immortal. I didn't remember the students, but I remembered the blood. It flowed like a river through the halls.

The depression that I had felt after the dream had closed over me like a casket. For weeks, I felt saddened by the lack of humanity, knowing somewhere deep inside of me that the dream had been real.

I nodded. "I've had enough to know that I'm not safe here."

His eyes turned into slits. "I'd like to know more of these dreams."

Tossing his words back to him, I said, "Perhaps tomorrow. Tonight is for celebrating."

I jerked out of his hold and began to weave my way through the crowd until I bumped into a kid that I vaguely remember from weapons training.

"Sorry," I said as he stabilized me from toppling onto the floor. *Damn high heels.*

"Hey, no worries. I've actually been meaning to talk to you. I'm Jase, by the way." He stuck out a hand, and I shook it.

"Gabriella."

"Yeah, I know," he said then blushed.

"So, what's up?"

"I'm fully blessed from Haniel's line."

I looked at his auburn hair and freckles. That made sense. "Oh, so cool. So is Hannah."

"Yeah," he said absentmindedly. "So, I get visions sometimes, you know. It doesn't mean that my visions come true. I actually don't tell people of them, because I get worried that I'll somehow change the future and make it worse, but ..." He squeezed the back of his neck as he looked down at his shoes.

I laid a hand on his arm. "Jase, you saw something bad, didn't you?"

He nodded.

"It involved me, didn't it?"

"Yeah, earlier today, I had a vision of you in that red dress, and you went out to get fresh air. That's why I've been standing at the doors. Someone hurts you bad." He coughed into his hand. "You don't make it."

Chills ran down my spine. "I died?"

He closed his eyes for a second and let out a groan. "See? I've just made it worse. They see you talking to me. They are going to spike a drink; offer it to you. You'll be dead by morning." He gripped my arm. "I can't see their faces. They were sent here, though, to destroy the fully blessed. It doesn't make sense though, because you're a demi. I have to go tell the commander. Come with me."

"I have to check on Hannah."

"Don't drink anything and stay by her side. I'll grab the commander."

I nodded then ran to find Hannah.

Anger rose inside of me. I tried to dial it back, but I was pissed. Someone planned on killing me tonight?

Hannah was still sitting at the table, eating her weight in lasagna, when I slammed my hand down on the table, startling her.

"I need to escape."

She looked worried for me. "But Gabriella—"

"Jase just witnessed my murder, Hannah. Someone is trying to kill me. If they don't succeed tonight, they will keep trying. I have to go."

Hannah's face turned paler than it normally was as she shook her head. "No. This is crazy. Please don't do this."

"I have to."

"Then I'll go with you."

"No." I stopped her from standing by placing a hand on her shoulder. "What if you're right, and we die by the time we're eighteen because some demon found us? I can't live with myself knowing that something happened to you."

Her eyes watered. "Yeah, well, I'm not letting you go by yourself. End of discussion. If you're going, then I'm going, too." She stood from the table. "Come on; we can slip out the back. I have an idea where the portal is. It's a total guess on my part, but it's all we got to go on right now."

I scanned the crowd for Remy and couldn't find her. She was going to be pissed that I left without telling her. I could feel in my gut that I would see her again, though. This was my chance. I had to take it.

"No one saw us," I said as I followed her outside, gathering the end of my dress in my hands.

I had to hand it to Hannah. For as tall and lanky as she was, she was silent on her feet as we headed for the shadowy woods.

My decision should have already been made once that woman, Sariel, had said I had been touched by more than one archangel. Then the commander had lied to everyone yet claimed it was to protect me. Now here I was, trying to escape my murderer.

Jase's words reverberated through me. I knew he was telling the truth. Just as I knew that, if I stayed on these grounds tonight, I'd be dead before the morning. I also knew that my dreams would soon come true.

No, I couldn't stay here. Something bad was coming. I could feel it.

I ran harder through the woods. As if Hannah could pick up on my anxiety, she ran faster, too. This was it. It was now or never.

thirteen

WE MOVED LIKE LIGHTNING THROUGH the dark forest. With one hand, I held the end of my dress up around my thighs so it wouldn't snag on the underbrush. With the other hand, I held my shoes. I could barely walk in high heels, much less jog through the forest at nighttime.

I tripped over a log that almost sent me sprawling. Luckily, I caught myself on my hands and knees.

Hannah helped me up. "Are you okay?"

"Nothing broken."

After twenty minutes of jogging, Hannah stopped at the edge of the forest and pointed between two trees. "While looking for wild ginseng one day, I found this. Do you see it? There is a small sliver that you can barely see in the full sun, so it's impossible to see now, but it's there. It looks like we have to climb up on the rock to the right and jump toward the tree on the left. It should exit us into the national park. There are wards all around the borders, so I'm guessing someone has been alerted by now. They will send a group of soldiers to check. We need to make it as far away from the border as we can."

This was my chance to escape, and I was going to take it.

I climbed up on the rock and jumped first, Hannah following me. With a thud, we landed in the national forest.

Not having time to take a break, we started to jog again, tripping over small branches and logs. My feet were a bloody mess when we finally stumbled out of the woods and onto a trail. Then we headed down the narrow dirt path, arm in arm. When the ground leveled out, we broke apart from one another. It was easier to run now without so many obstacles in our way. The cardio class had really paid off.

After what seemed like hours, we exited the trail to the empty parking lot.

Hannah rested her palms on her knees, gasping for air. "What do we do now?"

"We walk along the highway until we can't walk anymore, and then we find a place off the road to sleep for a bit before we start walking again."

Hannah stood tall, shoulders back. All six feet of her started walking like a woman on a mission. I couldn't have possibly loved her any more than I did at that moment.

At some point, we started stumbling from exhaustion,

and that was when I decided we needed sleep, if only for a few hours. There was a small barn off the side of the road. We could hunker down there until the morning, and then maybe we could bum a ride from someone.

We entered the barn, and I threw down my shoe, snorting as I realized this whole damn time I carried only one. I must've lost the other one a while back.

I pointed at some hay bales stacked neatly against a wall, too tired to talk.

Hannah gave me a nod. Taking a nap on the hay was a solid plan.

Before sleep could fully pull us under, there was a commotion outside the barn. My stomach clenched, and I knew that my gut was warning me that trouble was on the way. I barely had time to process that before two demons came strolling into the barn.

They could have passed for humans, unless you were up close with them, and that was exactly what Hannah and I were—up close.

Their eyes were black with the outer rim lined in red. When they smiled down at us with malice, we saw their sharp canines.

The taller man on the right reached out and snagged a curl of Hannah's hair. I reached out and slapped his hand, causing him to drop the curl.

"Oh, what do we have here? She's feisty. Just how I like them."

A rat scurried out from the bale of hay. Feeling a

connection with it as I did with all animals, I reached for that power that, up until this point, I kept suppressed and let it unwind. Making eye contact with the rat, I silently pleaded.

Its tiny head bobbed before it exited out of a hole in the barn wall.

Through the door that the demons had left open, there was a large tree that began to sway toward me.

The shorter, more muscular man laughed. "It was that one that got our attention."

"Yeah, girly, we were just cruising down the road when your light called to us. So bright. You must not know how to control it yet." He laughed. "And it just got brighter."

The shorter one asked, "Where were you girls coming from? Dressed all pretty-like. It doesn't make sense, does it, Akkadian?"

The other demon shook his head. "No."

"We were going to a party with our boyfriends. We decided to go our separate ways." Something in me stopped me from speaking of the academy.

The taller one crouched down in front of me. "That wasn't very smart. It will be our greatest pleasure killing someone with so much light."

The shorter one shook his head at me. "She has too much light. She's fully blessed."

"You think so?"

The other demon nodded while Hannah looked at me with shock.

"Well then, I guess this is going to turn into a real party. We get paid a pretty penny if we bring her in." He winked at me. "Dead or alive."

As he went to grab for me, a group of rats started to bite his ankles. Startled, he fell over backward. The rats squeaked as they quickly climbed up the trunk of his body.

Outside, the large tree was rocking so hard that I knew what was about to happen as I willed it to do so. I grabbed Hannah's hand and made a mad dash for the open door while commanding the rats to exit the barn. Out of the corner of my eye, I saw them scramble off the demon and hurry toward their hole.

The other demon was reaching for us just as the tree came crashing through the roof. Expecting it, I didn't stop, running as hard as I could while pulling a shocked Hannah behind me. The tree crashed down on the barn, flattening it, and I hoped the demons inside.

We stood in silence for a few seconds.

"Are they dead?" Hannah asked.

A sound came from the collapsed barn. Boards began to shift and move as a demon roared.

"Nope. I think we might have just made them angrier. We need to run."

Before I could turn around, strong arms encircled me.

Hannah's eyes bugged out, and her face, that was usually snow-white, somehow became even paler.

Whatever was behind me knew it had caught its prey, and as I began to struggle, the arms tightened around me.

How could I get out of this? This was my fault. My friend was going to die because of me.

The demons crawled out of the demolished barn with a look of fury until they saw my captor. Then the look was replaced with fear. I knew why as soon as I heard his voice.

fourteen

MY CAPTOR DROPPED HIS ARMS away from me before he pushed me out of the way. "Hello, boys."

My jaw dropped as the commander walked past me to stand in front of the demons that were currently backpedaling. "Thought you'd have a bit of fun, did you?"

"Oh, we didn't know they belonged to you," the shorter one almost whispered.

The taller one popped his neck side to side. "What is a fully blessed doing roaming the woods? It seems like she was begging for us to find her." He gave me a smirk before he made the horrible mistake of charging the commander.

The commander stood there with his arms by his sides, not even reaching for the huge sword strapped to his back. What was he thinking? Then, at the last second, he stepped to the left while cupping the demon under the chin with

his right hand. He spun in a half-circle until he was behind the demon, his left hand across the demon's forehead. In one motion, he jerked up on the demon's neck and twisted. The demon dropped to the ground, motionless, before I even registered what had just happened.

Hannah moved closer to me, and we gripped each other's hands as the commander very calmly walked to the other demon. As soon as he was in striking distance, the shorter demon decided to go down swinging, and that's precisely what happened.

The commander caught the demon's fist and twisted him around before he performed the same motion he had with the other demon. We heard the *crack* from where we stood, immobilized.

The Rocks, Dan and Richard, who we hadn't even noticed, came strolling forward.

The commander gave each of us a hard stare. "You might not want to watch this next part."

I hadn't wanted to watch the first part!

My eyes flashed to Dan and Dick before settling back on the commander. "Wh-what are they going to do?"

"Burn them to ashes." He grabbed my arm not so gently. "Let's go. Keep up, Hannah."

"Yes, sir," she said as she trailed behind us.

There was so much rage coming off the commander that I feared what he was going to do to us.

As the trees swayed like a tropical storm was coming, he barked, "Control your emotions."

"Trying."

"Try harder."

We walked until we came to the road. There, he pointed at a boulder on the other side. "Go wait there, Hannah."

She bit her lip nervously, looking from me to the commander, before she nodded.

As soon as she was a reasonable distance away, the commander roughly pulled me to face him. "What the hell were you thinking?"

My fear of the repercussions was replaced with a wave of white-hot anger. "I'll tell you exactly what was on my mind. You know those dreams you asked about? Well, yeah, I have them. I've had a lot of them, and I can promise you, buddy, that they don't paint the academy in a good light. Just the opposite, in fact. I've seen things. Like teenagers killing teenagers."

His brows came together.

"And tonight, Jase said he saw me dying. Since I've stepped onto this campus, I've felt Marlie-Beth's and Angelina's hate. Not dislike toward me, but genuine hate. What's with that? There are others, too, who must be pure darken, and then let's not forget your encrypted warning. You know, the one where you said my enemies could literally be anyone, including my best friends. You also lied to all the students, claiming you were trying to protect me."

"I was!" he boomed. "But you always make it so damn difficult."

"Always? What are you talking about?"

He shut his mouth.

My mind was boggled. When I had first met him, he acted as if it was I who was a ghost. The way he stared at me was almost haunting. Then he hadn't been shocked that I had been touched by more than one archangel.

Hands on my hips, I asked, "Do I know you?"

He took a step closer. "I think you'd remember me, wouldn't you?"

I ignored the heat in my belly. "And for the record, I knew without a shadow of a doubt that I would die tonight if I stayed at the academy."

He bent his knees so he could get eye level with me. "Let me make myself very clear. You should be scared. Your dreams and intuition are probably accurate. However, if you would have come to me, I could have protected you. Instead of trusting me though, you endangered not only your life but Hannah's, as well!"

He was right. I hadn't trusted him, and if I had, maybe the outcome would have been different.

"I'm sorry. I did what I felt was right at the time. If I hadn't been so tired, I could have hid my powers better, and the demons wouldn't have sensed us. I almost got my friend killed tonight."

He ignored my apology. "Trust me when I say you will not last a day out here in this mess. I'm surprised you lasted this long, to be honest with you. The minute you became exhausted, you became a beacon. That is how

I found you. To think you won't get tired again in the future is ludicrous. If you stay at the academy, I can help you, but I can't always be here to save you if you run." His green eyes were bright with anger but also with another emotion. He was genuinely worried.

He cleared his throat. "You didn't come to me because you don't trust me."

My heart clenched at the torment in his tone.

I avoided his eyes when I nodded.

"We need to fix that." He jerked me to him until our bodies were flushed, his arms a warm cocoon around me, yet I shivered.

I momentarily lost myself, forgetting what we were arguing about. Now that my fear and anger had faded, I could feel that tug in my belly. The one that alerted me when he was near and insisted that I get closer to him.

"I will find out who planned on hurting you, and I will end them. And, for future reference, don't ever scare me like that again. I don't like it."

I wet my lips, and his eyes tracked the motion. I swear he let out a low growl.

"How did you know that I went through the magical gateway?"

"There's only one way in and one way out. Plus, I found your shoe, Cinderella. I didn't need to hunt down everyone in the village to figure out whose foot it belonged on."

He let go of me so abruptly that I almost fell on my butt. The Rocks, Dan and Richard, had come up to stand beside him, and he gave them direction. Then he called a shell-shocked Hannah over to us. Before we knew it, we were heading back the way we had just come.

I dashed a tear away, numbly putting one foot in front of the other. Until I figured out how to permanently hide this light that the demons could obviously see, being out in the open wasn't safe or smart. I clearly saw that now. There was no way I was capable of killing two demons by myself. At least, not yet. But staying at the academy wasn't ideal, either. I could feel something bad about to happen. It was in the air, and it was only a matter of time before my dreams of the academy came true.

We were walking back up the trail when the adrenaline wore off, and the severity of what had almost happened hit me. I felt as if I was about to have a nervous breakdown when the commander dropped back down the trail to walk beside me.

Gruffly, he said, "I understand why you ran, just don't do it again. This time, there was no harm. You're fine, and Hannah is fine."

He went from wanting to murder me to attempting to comfort me? Strange man. What was even stranger was the gravitational pull I felt toward him every time he was near. Yes, he was the most beautiful male I had ever seen, but that wasn't the reason behind me wanting to be close to him. It was something else. Something that ran deep. It was a connection that I'd rather ignore than deal with. I currently had too much on my plate as it was.

"I'm sorry," I whispered, craning my neck to look up at him.

His green eyes bore into mine, causing my breath to hitch. Lost in the moment, I tripped over a root and barely had time to stumble before he snagged my arm, stabilizing me. Just when I thought he'd let me go, he kept his hand on my arm.

Feelings I couldn't understand or control were surfacing. I had barely met this man, yet I craved his touch.

"Here is something I can share. I need you to trust me. You are demonstrating higher power levels than most, and you haven't got the brunt of your gifts yet. Let the dreams come. Pray for them. Figure out all the answers to your questions. And if you allow me to help you, I'll train you so that, the next time you come across demons, you will be the one they fear."

"Can …? Can you tell me why I'm different than the others?" I asked.

"Yes. Do you think you can wait until tomorrow when we're both not exhausted and can think more clearly?"

He was right; I was drained. Exhaustion was wearing me down as we continued to walk back toward the academy.

I looked down at the hem of the red dress. It was the first dress that I had ever worn, and now it was completely ruined.

"You'll have more dresses," he said.

Unconsciously, my brows drew together. "Can you read my mind?"

"I wasn't reading your mind." He chuckled. "You were always just easy to read."

"There you go with that *always* again. Care to elaborate?"

"I could," he said, "but maybe this is something I want you to figure out all on your own."

I tripped again; this time on the hem of my dress that was coming unraveled.

The commander swung me up into his arms, saying, "Your feet are bloody," as a way of an explanation.

I started to argue. I mean, who could possibly carry someone in this position up a trail for more than an hour, which had only become steeper with every footfall? Well, the Rock, Dick, had thrown me over his shoulder like a sack of potatoes. Still … But the commander wasn't even wheezing, so I didn't say anything. I seriously doubted there was much that man couldn't do.

I let out an unladylike yawn, and then I laid my head on his chest. His breath hitched, making me think that maybe my feelings weren't just a one-way street, and that was the last thing I remembered before I took a much-needed nap.

I awoke the moment we crossed the veil. There, he placed me back on my feet and clasped my hand as he walked me to my dorm, while the Rocks walked a laughing Hannah to her room. Students were out and about, and everyone who saw me with the commander in last night's gown started talking. It would help if he let go of my hand, but I had decided after my little stunt that it was best not to argue with him right now.

Without a word, he escorted me directly to my room then left. I then changed out of the once beautiful gown and into an oversized T-shirt and crawled in my bed, thankful that Remy wasn't there to pester me with questions because I needed sleep.

fifteen

I SLEPT THE WHOLE DAY away, missing my opportunity to talk with the commander about my lineage, but that night, the dreams came.

The fifteen angels were in an abandoned house.

Ariel spoke up. "Our wings will always be black now."

"We made a mistake," Michael said. "One that we would probably repeat, but nonetheless, we've apologized and we're moving forward. We will display our wings with no shame."

There were a couple of nods.

Sandalphon gazed at his brothers and sisters. "There is something I'm not understanding. Lucifer and his tribe are no selfless good-doers; why did they leave their mark on the ones we touched?"

"More importantly. what will it do to them?" Ariel asked.

Raziel spoke up. "Technically, we carry the same label

as them—fallen—but we are very different than our dark brothers and sisters. Our power is still pure, no matter the color of our wings. We passed through hell to get to earth. We did not linger or choose to stay for a long period of time. Lucifer and the others are dark angels now." He paced in front of the archangels. *"We knew how much to give to each human in order to save them from the disease that spread. Yes, they have special little gifts now, like good immune systems or great intuition, that they'll pass down to their children, but other than that, they won't be altered."*

Gabriel gnawed on her lip. "But if the fallen ... the dark angels added their dark powers ... "

The room grew quiet.

"If the dark angels were powerful enough, their touch combined with ours ... well, it's going to turn those humans," Raziel said.

"Into what?" Ariel asked.

"Immortals."

Gabriel had known before this all started that something bad was going to happen, but in her wildest dreams, she never imagined that they would create something that should have never existed in the first place.

sixteen

THE NEXT MORNING, THERE WAS a knock on my door. I was drowsy as I got out of bed in my oversized T-shirt. Last night's dream had left me feeling haunted. I needed to find out what had happened to the humans and the archangels, and the only way to do it was to go back to sleep and hope the dreams came back. First, I had to get rid of the commander who was about to beat my door down.

I swung the door open to find him frowning down at me.

"You didn't show up to your first class today."

I had nothing to say, so I just shrugged and stared at his chest.

"Get dressed. I want to show you something." I started to argue, but he said, "You have five minutes. After that,

I'm coming back in to get you. So, get dressed. You can walk or be carried out of your dorm in that sad shirt you wear to bed."

I glared at him as he shut the door, but the moment it clicked, I changed into something else. All I needed now was to be paraded around campus in my Mickey Mouse shirt and panties.

I brushed my hair and teeth and was just sliding on my shoes when he entered my room … without knocking.

"Hello, privacy?"

"It's been five minutes," he said. "I'm a man of my word."

I begrudgingly followed him out of my room and building. We cut across campus and went behind a large building that held equipment for lawn care. Then we took a path through the woods where the trees were so thick that the sunlight barely came through the underbrush. Pretty and hella creepy at the same time.

Joking, I asked. "Are you planning my death?"

With a sexy grin, he looked over a shoulder at me. "You said something similar to me on testing day." His green eyes sparkled with amusement. "No, I'm not planning your death, but then again, I'm not much of a planner."

"Well, that's comforting."

"Glad I could help."

It was almost like we were flirting, but that would be insane, because the fierce warrior in front of me wouldn't do something so teenage-ish.

We kept walking down the path, and I tried not to ogle his butt, but dang it, Remy was right. It was super nice.

I sighed, thinking of my friend. I was pretty sure she was avoiding me. I had to find her after this and explain why I had run. If she would listen, that was.

The path eventually led us to a small lawn in front of a tiny cabin.

"This is where I live. I'm close to the school in case the students need me, but far enough away that I can have some peace and quiet when it's needed."

"Cool." *Why am I at his home?*

He opened the door, and I followed him, my eyes darting everywhere as I tried to get a glimpse of the commander's home and learn a little about who he really was.

The house was warm and friendly. There was a kitchen that flowed into the living room that had a tiny fireplace. Everything smelled of cedar and was neat and orderly. I expected nothing less of the commander.

He leaned a hip against the kitchen counter. "I know that you are upset, confused, and scared. This is normally a lot for students to take in without having someone try to murder them. I haven't been able to find out who it was, and Jase is not getting a visual on his end. I will make sure that you are safe here, though."

I dropped my gaze to my black sneakers that the academy had provided. To say I was a little embarrassed that he had come to my rescue yesterday was an understatement.

"I understand why you ran, but no matter what Jase's

visions are, you can't run off again. I have a suggestion."

"What's that?"

"A binding spell."

"Um … yeah, no offense," I said, "but I'm not really liking what that's implying."

He crossed his huge arms over his chest. Tattoos swirled around his biceps and down his forearms.

I swallowed hard and focused back on my feet. If I started drooling now, it'd be a hell of a lot more embarrassing than getting rescued from some demons.

"It's safe, Gabriella. It would join our emotions together, so I'd know if you were ever in trouble. It's also like a magical GPS; I could track you no matter where you went." Before I could say anything, he held up a hand. "I'll teach you how to block me out if you ever decided you wanted some emotional privacy, and this is also undoable. If you decide it's too invasive, we can have the binding removed."

I barely knew the commander, yet I trusted him. Still, I asked, "Can I think about it?"

He nodded. "Of course. Binding your emotions to someone is a big deal. Just keep in mind it could keep you alive."

He walked over to a bookshelf. "I know you have questions, and I want you to have answers. I have some priceless books and artifacts at my home that I won't turn over to the library. I would like for you to see them, to have a better understanding of the archangels—why they did what they did and what they are continuing to do."

I didn't say anything. My emotions were all over the place. The dreams of the angels were fresh on my mind. I needed to know what became of the blessed.

He ushered me to a couch, and I sat on the soft cushions, trying not to fidget.

"Would you like to know what I know about your lineage?"

I couldn't speak, so I just nodded as he sat down next to me, his thigh brushing up against mine.

"During a plague, a long time ago, angels healed humans. When they did that, it left an imprint on the humans they touched. Not a big deal. These humans would live normal lives, and their children would, as well. Their whole line would be called demis. If you watch the demis train or spar, you will notice that they are a tad quicker, more flexible, or can judge their opponent better than a normal human. That would have been fine, if Lucifer and his angels hadn't gotten involved."

My knee was frantically bouncing up and down. He reached out and squeezed it. When he removed his hand, I almost groaned from the loss of contact.

"So, what happened next?"

"The fallen, who we now refer to as the darken, have been on a mission ever since. They try to track down the blessed and give them some of their essence, too, to make the humans immortal."

"Why would they do that, though?"

His green eyes flashed, turning the emerald color a little darker. "Because the balance was off. Immortals should have never been created. Now demons can come from the underworld when they please. The archangels are fighting, but they are vastly outnumbered since a few of them have died."

"Wait—What? Angels can't die."

"Yes, by Azrael's blade, also known as the Flaming Sword. Which wouldn't have been a problem except Azrael lost his blade."

"How the hell did he lose a blade that can kill him?"

"In a battle. With the angels at war with each other and each group trying to get ahead of the other, it all came down to that sword. Whoever possessed it would have the advantage, because it is the only thing that can kill an angel.

"The archangels found a way to seal the underworld so that no more demons could come through, but they were still having to fight the darken, plus some of the blessed who have chosen the darken's side.

"Azrael protected the sword for centuries when, one day, him and his brothers and sisters were ambushed."

The hair on my arms rose. "What happened to them?"

"They had gathered together for a celebration." The commander had a faraway look in his eyes. "Word got out that all the archangels would be in the same place at the same time. They were all coming together for a girl who they all loved. That's when they were ambushed. With the sheer number of darken and demons that showed up, they were able to wrestle the sword away from Azrael.

"The battle raged in that small town, and when the darken and demons attacked the human girl, she got injured. Several of the archangels were injured, as well. Before they took their last breaths though, they blessed the girl. Seven archangels died that day."

"That's horrible. So that's how they lost the sword?"

"They only lost it for a few minutes. Of course, it killed seven archangels in those minutes."

"How'd they get it back?"

"The son of Lucifer got the sword back."

"Whoa. The *son* of Lucifer?"

The commander nodded as he stared off into space. "Yes, he was there for the celebration, as well. His powers were stronger than even the strongest archangel, Sandalphon himself. In his rage, he got the sword back. The darken ran off like the cowards they are, and the demons were slain.

"Azrael, in his grief of losing so many of his brothers and sisters, decided to hide the sword somewhere nobody would think to look. He knelt next to that human girl and poured the sword into her being. He put in enough power that she'd return again in a few centuries, giving her enough time that the darken wouldn't remember her. She took her last breath … and the sword with her."

An uneasy feeling settled upon me. "Commander, who was that girl?"

He finally looked at me, his green eyes holding an emotion that I couldn't quite decipher. "You, Gabriella.

The girl was you."

My whole world tilted.

He reached out to steady me with his warm hands. "Are you okay?"

I clenched my jaw. "As okay as any normal person would be after learning they had been reincarnated and carried some kind of angel killing sword in her body."

"It's important that you tell no one about this."

I glared at him. "You think? Do I look like I want to die again?"

As I sat there, my mind reeling, he stood and made his way to the kitchen. He came back a few minutes later with some food and a cup of warm tea.

"Eat," he commanded.

I picked up the bread and cheese and began to chew. I swallowed, even though the food felt like lead.

"I have a million questions."

"I'm sure you do." He reached out and tucked a stray piece of hair behind my ears. I tried to ignore the flush I felt over the simple touch. "Why don't you start with the hardest question?"

"Will I be hunted?"

His eyes turned a darker shade of green. I was beginning to recognize the deeper color meant he was angry. "Only if people find out. In that case, I'll kill them myself."

My hands shook as I took a sip of tea. "Which archangels touched me?"

"Azrael, Gabriel, Ariel, Raphael, Uriel, Jeremiel,

Chamuel, and possibly Haniel. They should have been able to heal you, but since you had been stabbed with the Flaming Sword, their powers, even combined, were not enough."

"Are they the same ones who died?"

He shook his head, his black hair falling across his forehead. "Azrael and Ariel did not die. Zadkiel did not touch you that day, but he perished in the fight.

"As Haniel was dying, she fell close to you, her hand grazing you before you took your last breath, so it's assumed that she poured the last bit of her power into you, as well. Gabriel's wound was superficial, but instead of choosing to heal herself, she chose to pour her remaining power into you."

"Why? That makes zero sense. An angel sacrificing themself for a human? What am I missing?" I cradled the hot cup in my hands, praying that some of its warmth would seep into my bones. "This is a lot to take in."

"I know. There is someone that I can ask to come here and talk with you. I think he would be able to answer a lot of your questions." He tapped the book on my lap. "Why don't you read about the academies and, while you're taking a break from the hard stuff, I'll go make that call; see when my friend can come to talk with you."

I still had so many questions, but he was right; I needed a break. I felt overwhelmed. "Thank you, Commander."

His smile was beyond compare. "You can call me Finn when we're not in school."

I cleared my throat. "Thanks, Finn."

He was quiet for a few seconds before he dismissed himself from the living room.

I read until my back grew sore from hunching over. I learned mostly about the archangels, the true defenders of the human race, and a little about the fallen, the darken. My eyes were growing heavy as I closed the book and stood.

Finn immediately offered me supper, but I declined. I didn't want him to think I was a complete charity case all the time.

"See you tomorrow after your last class," he said sternly. "No more skipping."

"Sure. Thanks."

My hand was on the door when Finn said, "Gabriella, please think about the binding. With everything that I've told you, I'm hoping that you'll understand how important it is to keep you safe."

I gave him a nod before I shut the front door. He was right; I already felt as if I was being hunted. If anyone knew what I possessed inside my body, I would forever be hunted. The darken and their army of demons would be after me, and I had a feeling they wouldn't stop until my head was mounted on a wall.

I was lost in my thoughts as I slowly walked back down the path and across the field toward the cafeteria. I nervously looked around, but no one was paying me any attention, yet I felt like there were eyes on me. I'd learned over the years to rely on my gut. I then noticed

Dan following me at a distance. The commander must have told them to keep tabs on me until he could convince me to do the binding spell.

Truth was I needed to learn as much as I could and quickly. I would start paying attention in Archangels 101, and even though I had never been a fan of the dreams, I might have to start taking naps during the day.

seventeen

THE NEXT MORNING, I DID my best to listen to every single word Mrs. Fields said. I was getting remarkably better in my hand-to-hand training class. Weapons class was still not my favorite, so I was glad when the bell rang, announcing it was officially lunch.

I grabbed my lunch tray and made my way over to my favorite tree. I looked around for Remy, but she was obviously still pissed at me for leaving the academy without telling her. It was clear that she was avoiding me.

Halfway to my tree, I noticed "the crew" had backed one of the newbies up against the corner of the building that housed the cafeteria. There, between the shrubberies, I overheard Marlie-Beth say, "Devon! Level one power; can you believe it? Why are they even allowing her to stay here? She is just tying up a room and wasting the teachers' time."

I seriously doubted she cared one way or another about the school funding.

She continued to murmur a couple of hateful remarks, her blonde hair swinging with every word. She was clearly beyond upset because someone who she considered a nobody dared to go and breathe the same air as her. What a joke.

I kept walking, telling myself, "Not my monkeys, not my circus," when Devon's next words stopped me in my tracks.

"Why don't me and the boys teach her a lesson?"

I looked back over to where a small crowd was now gathering. A couple of boys were giving each other high-fives, and the poor girl they had backed against the wall looked like she was going to barf at any moment.

I scanned the area to see if any teachers were going to intervene, but they all seemed to be busy—whether it was on purpose or not, I couldn't say. I felt my shoulders sag, knowing that I was only about to make things worse for myself.

I put on my determined face and started marching over to the corner of the building. Out of the corner of my eye, I saw Richard heading toward me. I gently gave him a shake of my head. I wanted to handle this, but knowing that he was there in case I needed him made me feel braver.

I didn't even recognize my own voice when I said, "Excuse me. How about we all quit acting like assholes and let the poor girl go?"

Marlie-Beth sneered. "Why? What are you going to

do about it? You think just because you're screwing the commander that you can get away with talking to me like that?" She laughed hysterically. "Devon, please handle her."

"I'm so confused," I said. "Is he your bitch?"

The terrified girl still in Devon's grip shook her head side to side, trying to warn me, but if I got my ass kicked, I wanted to go out in style.

Devon relaxed his hold on the freshman long enough for her to squeeze past him. She spared me an appreciative glance before high-tailing it out of there, for which I didn't blame her one bit.

I turned around, trying to make a hasty retreat myself, but found myself walking into a brick wall. One of Devon's friends stood in front of me with a smile on his face. I thought he was grabbing my tray to steady it, so that the mashed potatoes and gravy didn't go all over his collared shirt, but that wasn't the case. He grabbed the tray and slung it onto the grass. I gave a little sigh at the wasted food and braced myself for what was going to come next.

He brought a lock of my hair up to his face and inhaled deeply. "I don't think we have ever been properly introduced; they call me Fridge because I am unmovable."

I thought it would be best if I just kept my mouth shut. I tried to sidestep him, only for him to block my exit with a beefy arm.

"Well, now, that's not very nice. I don't think our conversation is over yet."

I heard Devon and the others laughing behind me, as I

saw Remy flying toward me, all mama bear. She came to a screeching halt an inch away from the beefy guy standing in front of me.

"What do you want me to do?" Remy asked at the same time the beefy guy leaned in really close to me, as if he were about to kiss me, while he moved his hands up my rib cage.

Ignoring Remy, I braced myself and prayed my aim was perfect. Then, raising my knee, I rammed him as hard as I could in the groin.

Unmovable my ass. He hit the ground hard.

I moved around him to head back to the open courtyard where more people were starting to gather to watch the show. The trees began to blow, not because there was wind, but they were picking up on my frightened state. Not that anyone noticed. They were all busy staring wide-eyed at the boy who was groaning in pain.

"I'll get you for that," the boy groaned out as Devon tried to help him back up to his feet.

Remy cheered, "Thatta girl!" She pointed a finger at the whole group. "You little shits just wait. I'm going to make all your lives miserable."

Marlie-Beth crossed her arms over her chest as she gave me a calculated look. I gave her a wink as I walked away. I passed a pissed-off Richard, who was stalking toward the group. I said a silent prayer that he would rip them all a new one.

Hannah met me as I was entering the cafeteria. She

grabbed my hand while she balanced her tray in the other. "I caught the tail end of the that from the lunch line." She glared at all the students who were staring at me. "Come on; let's go to your room. We can share my food."

Now that my adrenaline wasn't pumping anymore, I felt like crying. That could have gone really bad.

Remy moved swiftly beside us, not bothering to go around students, as she passed right through them. They must've felt the strange energy that swept through them, but not being able to see Remy, they all just gave me a weird look.

Remy was pacing as I reached a hand out to her and said, "I'm sorry. Please forgive me?"

She started to say something when Hannah said, "What? That wasn't your fault. Don't be ridiculous."

Remy rolled her eyes at Hannah, even though it wasn't her fault that she couldn't see my ghost bestie.

As soon as we entered my room, I sat cross-legged on my bed and put my head in my hands. This place sucked.

Hannah put her tray down on the only desk in the room then sat next to me, rubbing a comforting hand over my back. "It'll get easier."

"Ha," Remy said as she continued to pace our tiny dorm floor. "No, it won't. Then again, what do I know? I'm just the chick who got murdered." She kicked the end of her old twin bed, causing it to move an inch.

Hannah's orange eyebrows lifted to her hairline. "Um, what the hell was that?"

I pointed to where Remy stood with her hands on her hips. "My roommate, Remy. She's a ghost."

Hannah's eyes grew wide as she stared too far to the right of where Remy actually was, causing Remy to roll her eyes. "Um … First, you don't tell me that you spent the morning with the commander, and now you're saying that you can communicate with the dead?"

"What do you mean, you spent the morning with the commander?" Remy shrieked. "I am five seconds from cutting a bitch. This is clearly best friend material here, and I am so tired of being shafted. I swear someone better start talking and soon."

"Yeah," I said to Hannah, "Remy's also temperamental."

Looking at Remy, I said, "I'm sorry for a lot of things." Then I quickly explained what Jase had said the night of the ceremony, and I told her about the demons that me and Hannah had come across. "And I spent the morning with the commander because …" What could I say? "Well, he thinks that maybe more than one archangel touched me, and he's worried what that could do for my safety. He wants to perform a binding spell so he can keep tabs on me."

Remy's blue eyes flared. "You are moving way too fast for me. I'm still stuck on the part where you left your BFF. Thank God I didn't get matching tattoos with you. Total waste of ink, biotch."

I looked over at Hannah, who was just staring wide-eyed, gaping at me and then the empty space.

Remy laughed. "And apparently, orange-is-the-new-red

here is stuck at me being a ghost."

"Yeah, listen. guys. I'm sorry. I'm sorry that I left and almost got Hannah killed by demons, and I'm sorry I haven't been a great friend. Forgive me?"

Remy rolled her eyes multiple times. "No need to be dramatic, but I do appreciate the groveling."

I laughed at my crazy-ass friend then looked at Hannah who was still zoned out. "It's important that you don't tell anyone about me being able to communicate with the dead. Also, we can't tell anyone about me being touched by more than one angel."

"Okay." Hannah's eyes were roaming the room frantically, as if she was still unsure of being in the same room as a ghost. Her shoulders were rigid as she sat there, trying to act like she was cool with it all. "So, let's talk about this ghost for a second."

Remy came to sit next to me, and as soon as her leg brushed up against mine, Hannah screamed, "I can see her!"

"Wait—what?" Remy said. She hopped off the bed and stood right in front of Hannah, waving a hand in front of her face.

"Where did she go?" Hannah asked.

Remy looked at me with disappointment.

Was Hannah able to see her because we had been touching?

I stood up and grabbed Remy's hand.

Hannah covered her mouth with her hands. "I can see her again."

Remy's blue eyes met mine. "Your touch gives others the power to see me. I can be real again!"

I smiled. "Yeah, Pinocchio, you're a real girl."

Remy held up a hand. "Shut it. This is no time for jokes."

Hannah's orange curls bounced up and down with excitement. "I can see a ghost! I can hear her, too!"

"Wait," I said, "you can *hear* her?"

"I like big butts," Remy said.

Hannah's long nose scrunched up. "Dude, not needed info."

Remy clapped her hands. "Oh, this is great. I mean, I think it's great."

"Why wouldn't it be?" I asked.

"Okay, so I've been going through Mrs. Fields' notebooks when she's asleep, like Nancy Drew asked me to," Remy began.

"That's not really what I asked of you," I said.

"Do you want to hear what I found out or not?" Without waiting for a reply, Remy continued, "So, apparently, the Empowered Academy takes in the fully blessed who are for the darken side. Well, there is a deal amongst the demons that, if they come across what looks to be a human that has a brilliant light, they are to bring the person to the Empowered Academy for a huge finder's fee. You, my friend, are high up on the power chain. If anyone knows that you have this kind of power, you'll be kidnapped or dead. Demons would be all over that shit."

"That's what Finn said."

An overplucked eyebrow rose. "You're on a first-name basis with hotness?"

"Wait—the demons that night said you were fully blessed; are you?" Hannah asked. "I mean, how else are you able to do these things? Most of us don't have powers like this until we're eighteen. I'm so confused."

I shrugged. "I'm demi, but I guess because I've been touched by more than one archangel, it's given me a leg up."

Remy waved an arm above her head. "Guess who read a journal about the blessed from Mrs. Fields' nightstand? Here's a hint: she's adorbs, totally dreamy, and if she were non-transparent, she would be a walking fashionista."

Hannah said, "Is she always like this?"

"Yep."

"Whatever," Remy scoffed. "So, listen up, my little freak and carrot top, this is what I've learned. There is a huge beef between our commander and theirs. It was implied that the Empowered Academy will do whatever it takes to make sure that this academy doesn't retain high-level blessed. That's probably why I was killed, and it's probably why you were being targeted, Gabriella. I'm not sure if anyone truly bought that whole you're-a-demi-but-we-don't-know-from-which-line spiel that the commander gave us.

"I don't know how the darken get ahold of the students here. It's all hush-hush and, to be honest, I don't think that old bat, Mrs. Fields, knows, either. I read every piece of paper regarding the academies that she had in her room and her classroom, and then I drew penises in all of the journals." She lifted one shoulder. "I was bored, and it was fun."

Hannah pulled her curly hair back from her face and tied it up. "This is so deep. I've been here for almost two years, and I've never heard of anyone that could see ghosts or knew that the feuds between the academies was leaking behind these walls and killing kids here. I feel like I've stepped into a soap opera with freakishly hot supes walking around, hoarding dirty little secrets."

Remy giggled. "That sounded more porn-ish. And to be fair, I think there has only been two students to die—a boy died a day before I did. So, maybe the commander has a hold on things now."

"How, though?" I asked. "Literally all is welcome here. There is no way to tell who is evil and who isn't."

There was a knock on my door.

"We'll talk later," I said. "But remember not to tell anyone about this ability or my abnormalities."

Remy pointed a stern finger in Hannah's face. "These pouty dead lips are sealed, so she's talking to you, my freakishly large, fascinating giraffe."

Hannah rolled her eyes. "I think I liked it better when I couldn't hear her. Of course I'm not going to say anything." Poor Hannah looked confused, scared, and excited all at the same time.

Whatever was going on at the academy was more than

either of us could probably handle.

When there was another knock, I dropped Remy's hand and opened the door. Trev stood there, leaning against the jamb, sporting a black eye.

"Hey, beautiful. Heard you were back."

Remy appeared behind Trev. She narrowed her eyes before she turned to me, holding a finger over her mouth.

"What happened to your face?" I asked.

He touched his left eye that was almost completely shut. "Oh, this? The commander said he slipped. That guy is such a prick. What did I ever do to him? Besides trying to look for you when you disappeared? He gave me an order to head back to campus, and I declined."

Remy gasped in horror. "How dare the hotter male mark this fine specimen's face? Does the commander know no boundaries? Also, does goldilocks here know about how you and my new pet giraffe almost got killed?"

I shook my head at Remy but remained eye contact with Trev. "It looks like it's just not our week."

He smiled. "You're telling me. I heard what happened." He shuffled his feet. "Why didn't you tell me what a student had envisioned?" I could see the hurt on his face.

Biting my lip, I said, "I panicked. All I could think about was running. I'm sorry."

Remy went to pass him, but then she poked her head back into our room. "I'm focused on the grass that is under that hot commander's feet, so I no longer care if goldilocks here goes commando. However, if the info of his undergarments or lack of just happened to fall in my lap, I wouldn't turn away such juicy gossip."

I hid my smile as I watched her float down the hall. My girl had issues.

"So, what's up?"

He raised his eyebrows at Hannah, who casually sat on the bed. He gave her a mock bow. "I was going to see if you wanted to walk to the next class together?"

"Um, sure."

I looked over at Hannah. "You know that conversation we had earlier, can we finish it tonight?"

She crossed her arms over her chest. "I wouldn't have it any other way. Meet you back here around three?"

I had to meet Finn around then. "How about five-ish?"

She gave me a thumbs-up as she hopped off my bed then squeezed past Trev.

I shut the door behind me, taking a deep breath and trying to act like everything was normal.

As we walked, his shoulders began to relax. I joked with Trev on the way to magic class and thought about how I needed answers, and I wasn't leaving Finn's until I had a few.

For whatever reason, I felt like I was in quicksand, slowly losing a battle that I wasn't even aware of why I was in it to begin with.

eighteen

THE WHOLE REST OF THE day at school went without incident. The crew left me alone, which was a Godsend in itself. Trev asked me a couple of times if I was okay and, each time, I just nodded. I was good as could be expected. He wanted to know what had happened when I was outside of the academy, and his face turned to stone when I told him of the demons, though he tried to pretend he wasn't upset that I left and was attacked.

He then asked how the commander found me so fast, and I just shrugged. I couldn't tell him that I had some kind of beacon inside of me. That would be confessing I was manifesting into my powers more quickly than I should have been. Powers that I technically shouldn't have, considering I was a demi. He didn't seem satisfied with my answer, but he let it go.

The day seemed to drag by. I tried so hard to focus on all my classes, but my mind kept wandering back to one question. *Why me?* Why would seven archangels, possibly eight, try to pour energy or their essence or whatever it was into me?

After all my classes were over, I made my way down the hall, in a hurry to get to Finn's. The commander would have answers for me.

I ran straight into a warm body.

"*Umph.*"

Trev laughed. "Where are you going to in such a hurry?"

"I have an additional class with the commander."

He narrowed his brown eyes. "Do you and the commander have something going on?"

"Like romantically? Um, no. Plus, I'm sure there are rules against those type of things. I mean, he's the commander here."

"He seems really into you, though."

"Yeah, well, we don't have anything going on."

I could tell he was still confused as to why Finn would give me special attention, but I couldn't speak of my lineage or how I was literally the freaking Flaming Sword. Therefore, I found myself hedging the truth.

"Because I'm so different, you know. They haven't figured out which line I come from, which is unheard of. Supposedly, this is the first time Sariel has ever been confused. I think he is trying to help me find out who I am."

He clenched his jaw. "Why are you meeting him at his place? Why not in a classroom at school?"

Why was it his business? Was he jealous?

"He has some items that might give us answers, but he doesn't like those items to leave his place. He's very particular."

Trev snorted. "I have some downtime; let me walk you to his place."

I started to argue, but that path was long and secluded, and after the confrontation that I'd had with the crew, it was probably in my best interest to not go anywhere alone.

"Sure. That'd be great," I said as a I hefted my heavy bag over my shoulder.

As we walked out of the building and toward the commander's house, I tried to start a conversation several times but, although he was smiling and nodding, I could tell he wasn't really listening. Finally, we came upon the commander's cabin. Thankfully, no one had tried to ambush us along the way.

I turned to Trev to thank him when he closed the distance between us and put one finger under my chin, tilting my face up to his. His voice was low as his eyes searched my face. For what? I didn't know. "I need you to know that I like you. Like, *really* like you."

I was in shock. I didn't know what to say. I had been thrown into this world with so many unanswered questions, and then there was the brooding commander that I felt a crazy kind of chemistry toward. Of course I thought Trev was hot. Who wouldn't? But I guessed, with all the chaos surrounding me, I hadn't thought of him in a boyfriend kind of capacity.

Now he was lowering his lips to mine. Was he going to kiss me?

I put my hands on his chest to create some space between us. Did I want him to kiss me?

I felt the heat tug in my belly, alerting me that Finn was nearby, and all of a sudden, being in Trev's arms didn't feel right.

My eyebrows came together in confusion when I heard a door opening then a voice clearing. I backed away from Trev to see Finn standing in the open door, his shoulders so wide that he took up all the space. He was staring at me with a look of disappointment that left me feeling guilty when I had nothing to feel guilty over.

"Um ..." I said to Trev. "Thanks for walking me here. After what happened today at lunch, it made me feel better."

I wasn't sure if he had heard me, since he didn't ask what had happened at lunch. Instead, he said, "No problem. Anytime."

Finn crossed his arms over his chest. "How's the eye?"

Trev didn't respond; he just stood there, staring at the commander. Then he looked at me and winked with his good eye. "I'll see you around, beautiful."

I watched as he walked back down the path, whistling a happy tune.

The commander cleared his throat as he stepped to the side, letting me into his home. He grabbed my bag from my shoulder, balancing it with two fingers, easily holding the weight that I had been straining under. "So, you two are an item?"

Didn't Trev just ask me something similar a minute ago?

I studied Finn as he moved silently into his living room, dropping my bag by the couch before he started to build a fire, even though it wasn't cold outside. He was stunning with his midnight black hair and piercing green eyes. He was a little taller than Trev, and just a tad bit more muscular. And, where Trev looked like an Abercrombie model, this man looked like he belonged on the cover of a romance novel, wearing nothing but a kilt.

I mentally slapped myself for comparing the two. I didn't have time to notice one boy, much less two.

He must have felt my eyes on him, because he looked at me from over his shoulder. I was grateful he hadn't seen me giving him a once-over a second ago. Just thinking about the possibility made my cheeks grow warm.

"No, Trev and I are just friends," I finally answered.

"It didn't look that way."

"With all due respect, Commander, it's not really your business, is it?"

He grunted. "I overheard you say that something happened to you during lunch today. What happened?"

I quickly told him of Devon and the rest of the crew.

His eyes smoldered before he said, "This is why we should do the binding. I could have felt your panic.

"I have a feeling it will not get easier for you. When you turn eighteen, it'll be even harder for you to hide your powers. The ones that have decided to be on the darken's side will know that you are special."

I gave him a nod. I was on the same page. However, just being bound to someone sounded equally as scary as being hunted by the darken. Okay, well, maybe not equally, but it was definitely terrifying to think the commander would be able to read all of my emotions. I felt a blush start to creep up my cheeks.

He cocked his head to the side and stared at me as I began to worry my lip between my teeth.

"Just give me until tomorrow to make a decision about the whole binding thing, okay?"

He stood slowly, and I raked my eyes over the length of him. Total perfection was what the commander was.

I rolled my eyes. *Great.* I was lusting after the teacher. That was definitely not good.

The commander let out a low laugh. "I'd love to be privy to your thoughts for a day."

Yeah, and he would be if we bound our souls together.

"Gabriel's journal is on the couch right next to you. Start reading."

I grabbed the book and put it in my lap. A jolt of longing ran through me as I touched the cover. Then I flipped it open and wiggled into a better position.

"Commander—er, Finn? Before I start reading, I thought maybe I should tell you that something a little strange happened to me today."

Without looking at me, he asked, "What's that?"

I told him about my friend Hannah and how she was able to see Remy when I was touching her.

He let out a sigh that was more like a groan. "So, Hannah knows that you've come into some pretty impressive powers?"

I nodded. "Sorry. But no one else will know. Plus, the demons that attacked me and Hannah were already talking about a light that I gave off, so she'd figured it out eventually."

He nodded. "You giving the dead life is actually not strange at all."

"It's not?"

"No, in fact, your powers will be way bigger than that." His gaze was intense. "I want you to be a fighting machine by the time anyone knows exactly who you are. It's extremely important that you don't tell anyone else about any of this. Understand?"

"I've only told Hannah, who's super cool, and Remy, who is a ghost, so I think we're safe."

"You didn't tell your boyfriend?"

"He's not my boyfriend, and no, I didn't. I have so many questions, though—"

I stopped speaking as the air in the room began to

intensify. A strong power washed over me before the back door was opened.

He didn't seem to be alarmed. Actually, he seemed to be excited as a man walked through the hall toward us, a blinding light surrounding him.

I put a hand up to shield my eyes as he stopped a couple of feet away from Finn. Then my mouth dropped open as I stared at what had to be a legit angel.

He was tall like Finn and just as muscular. In fact, they could have been cousins, if it wasn't for their coloring. I knew immediately who I was staring at.

"Sandalphon?"

He smiled at me, causing me to cringe. "Sorry. Let me turn down the brightness. Normally, people tend to not see the light, but it seems that you're special."

Within seconds, I was able to gaze upon him without wincing. He was absolutely magnificent.

"Ella, it's been a long time."

"Um ..."

Finn cleared his throat. "This is Gabriella."

"Oh, I'm sorry, of course."

That was super strange. What was even more bizarre was the way Finn was gently shaking his head at Sandalphon.

They stared at each other for several minutes, as if they were having a silent conversation. Then Sandalphon gave Finn a sad smile before nodding.

Obviously, something was up.

"So, Gabriella," the angel started, "it's very nice to

officially meet you."

"Do you know me?" When he looked over to Finn again, I said, "You were one of the ones who fought against the darken the day that I died. The day that I became the Flaming Sword."

He gave a solemn nod. "I lost seven brothers and sisters that day. We all lost something that day."

Sandalphon then changed gears, grabbing Finn up in a bear hug. "Hey, my boy, how are you doing?"

Finn smiled. "Like you don't know."

Sandalphon stroked his five o'clock shadow. "It's true; I might keep tabs on you."

"You both have similarities," I blurted.

Sandalphon laughed. "It's because I am the one who blessed him."

They both smiled at that.

I watched as the angel stood there, laughing with Finn and catching up just like a father and son would.

Finn then turned to me with a smile on his face. "Gabriella, this is who I called to talk with you, but before he does, I have some business to go over with him. Can you sit tight and read for a second, and we will be right back?"

"Sure."

I watched as they walked into the dining room that was off the kitchen. I could still see them, but I couldn't hear what they were saying. Both men looked a lot alike, but Finn didn't have fair hair or blue eyes. I had seen that shade of green somewhere before …

While they continued to talk, I picked up a different book from Finn's collection, one that was based on the fifteen archangels. I flipped through it until I came across Gabriel. Her eyes were beautiful, but they didn't look like jewels that were cast from the heavens. I ran a hand over her image. I could have been her twin—same dark hair, blue eyes, and full lips.

I flipped the page to Ariel. Remy didn't look like the blonde angel, but she did share the same electric eyes.

There was no doubt that Hannah got more than a few attributes from the angel Haniel. That orange, wiry hair and pale skin was a dead giveaway that Hannah had been touched by Haniel.

As Sandalphon and Finn slowly made their way back into the living room, I asked, "Hey, question. So, I noticed that whatever line we come from, we have some of that angel's characteristics. Why do some of the blessed carry a heavier resemblance than most?"

It was Sandalphon who answered. "In the beginning, when the archangels came across the sick, they blessed them to help heal their frail bodies. The sicker the human was, the more of the angel's essence was poured into them. After they were healed, they tended to favor the angel with a few characteristics."

"But I look a lot like Gabriel. Like, carved from the same stone."

"You do." Sandalphon came to sit next to me, his fist clenched in his lap. "Angels weren't made to fall in love, but Gabriel was the closest thing to love that I ever felt. She struggled with the fall from heaven. She needed something in her life to focus on, other than besting Lucifer and the rest of the darken. She was the only archangel to sleep with a human and produce an heir."

I gasped. "She had a baby?"

He reached out and squeezed my knee. "Yes, you, my dear."

I looked over at Finn, who had propped himself up against a wall. His arms, with those corded muscles, were crossed over his chest. He gave me a tight nod. "You're Nephilim, Gabriella. I could have told you all this, but Sandalphon said, when the time came to tell you who your mother was, he wanted to be the person to share the news. Him and your mother were as close as two angels could be."

Sandalphon said, "None of us ever knew your human father. Gabriel never spoke of him, but it was clear that you took after him in the way that you viewed things. That seemed to please Gabriel, who adored humans. She didn't want any of us to bless you, because she never wanted you to be hunted by the darken. We all agreed, and each one of us enjoyed watching over you. You became everyone's niece. Everyone's pride and joy.

"After long days, weeks, months of fighting the darken, we would come back to check on your mother and her little miracle. *Our* little miracle." He smiled while reminiscing. "I remember how much mischief you seemed to always be in. Your childhood went by so fast. In a blink, really. So, naturally, the day came when you left home to start your own life, and we all tried to give you the space that you needed. Poor Chamuel really struggled with that. He was more overprotective than even I.

"Not a year went by after you left before your village was attacked." His eyes shone brightly. "I know this life hasn't been easy, Gabriella, but know that, in your past life, you had so many who loved you. A mother who sacrificed herself to save you."

A tear streaked down my face. "I want to remember."

He laid a hand on my shoulder. "Then dream of it soon."

"Why was I in foster care? If I still have aunts and uncles who love me, why didn't they raise me when I was re-born?"

A sad look crossed his face. "We didn't know when you would be coming back to us, and the truth is I wouldn't let anyone search for you. The darken would have found you. If we had taken an interest in you, they would have taken an interest in you. Believe it or not, you were safer without us knowing where you were."

I gave him a tight nod. I understood what he was saying, but it didn't mean that it sucked any less. Then again, I was apparently loved before and had had a good life, yet I had ended up dead, so there was that.

He stood slowly and walked over to Finn. "I'm glad you called me. I have been wanting to check on you." He placed a hand on Finn's shoulder. "I know this wears heavily upon you. It wears heavily on us all. If the darken find out that she is the Flaming Sword, they will take her, my boy. Have your guard up, son."

Fear trailed down my spine. The thought of being hunted by the darken was enough to make me sweat.

Finn gave the angel a nod. "Always."

The angel made a gesture between us. "Well, I'll let the both of you get back to … whatever it was that you were doing before I showed up."

Finn walked the angel out of the cabin, and when he returned, the mood had changed. Finn was even more distant than usual.

Without saying a word, he started pushing the furniture back.

"What are you doing?" I asked.

"You are the only person who has ever been directly born from any of the fifteen archangels. You are also the only one who has been blessed by multiple angels." He stopped rolling the rug and walked toward me, only stopping when he was right in front of me. He put a hand on my chest, and at his warm touch, I almost stopped breathing. "Inside of you is more power than anyone could ever fathom. You, Gabriella, carry the Flaming Sword inside of you. I want you to stop using your mind so much and start fighting with your heart."

I took a deep breath, my chest rising, pressing into his palm.

I watched as his eyes darted to my lips before he cleared his throat and took a step back. Then he continued rolling up the rug then moved it to the side of his living room.

He stood in the middle, telling me, "They have given you so much. Learn to fight so that it wasn't all for nothing."

He was right.

This time when we fought in the middle of his living room, I gave it everything I had. He didn't go easy like Trev did. No, he wasn't satisfied until every muscle in my body ached, and I couldn't physically get back to my feet. I took several minutes laying on his rug, just catching my breath, a smile on my face. I had gotten two hits on the mighty commander. A roundhouse kick to the shoulder and an uppercut to the stomach that almost broke my hand, but still. With both hits, he had given me a smile that was worth a thousand words.

When I groaned as I sat up, he laughed then threw a water bottle at me. It was time for me to head back to my dorm and take a hot shower.

On shaky legs, I made my way to his door, where he refused to let me carry my own bag. He just served me my ass over and over again yet carried my bag for me as he escorted me back to my dorm. Before he left me, he commanded me to have dreams, and that I did.

nineteen

THAT NIGHT, I SMILED AS the dream I had hoped for came to me. Like a movie on the screen, I watched the archangels like they were my favorite characters.

They watched over those who they had blessed, but it was one child in particular that had caught their interest. They cooed over the child with her cherubic cheeks and twinkling blue eyes that were an exact replica of her mother's. As she grew from a toddler to a teen, they all popped in on her and her doting mother.

I watched in fascination as the beautiful angel, Gabriel, dressed the now young woman, Gabriella—me—in an ivory gown with lace. Her eyes misted over as she braided my hair, tucking dandelions into the braid.

I laughed. "Mom, wouldn't roses be more fitting for my wedding day?"

"No, daughter. Roses have certain conditions in which they can grow. A dandelion, though, can grow through hard clay. It is resilient and beautiful, just like you."

I grabbed her hand and squeezed. "Thank you for helping me get ready."

"There is nowhere that I'd rather be, daughter of mine." Her eyes met mine. "Can I just say that I never thought that anyone would ever be worthy of my daughter until I met my future son-in-law. He is perfect."

A grin split my face. "And so handsome he must be an angel."

We both laughed. Then I stood and walked toward the door that held my future, my happiness.

One minute, I was dreaming of an upcoming wedding and a love between a mother and daughter, and in the next, the dream faded away from them and turned darker.

Camaella was screaming in pain, begging to be released from the torture. She vowed to do anything.

At that simple yet powerful word, Lucifer appeared. He gently stroked her soggy red hair from her face, but with every touch, more pain was brought to her. The more she wept, the more he laughed.

twenty

I WAS SITTING IN CLASS, stewing over last night's dream. I had a mom at one time. A mom who had loved me. A mom who had been an archangel. I chewed on the end of my eraser. Had I made it through my wedding day before I was slaughtered?

What would happen if the darken found out that someone like me existed? They wouldn't kill me. Not if I was the Flaming Sword. They would use me to take out as many blessed as they could.

Anxiety ran through my veins and panic had swelled up inside of me by the time Hannah sat down in the desk next to mine. Her pale skin looked flushed from running to get to class before the bell rang. Her flaming orange, unruly curls stood up in every which way. Something was wrong.

"Hey, are you okay?" I asked.

She shook her head. "This morning, two of the girls from the crew cornered me at my lockers."

"It's because you're friends with me?"

"Does it matter?"

"It does to me."

"They are overly obsessed with you. They wanted to know why you were going to the commander's personal quarters."

"What did you say to them?"

"I didn't tell them that you were learning about the angels who had touched you, if that's what you're asking. I told them that you sucked at hand-to-hand combat, and the commander said he would catch you up, which isn't a total lie. Then Marlie-Beth slammed me into my locker and asked me when your birthday was."

"What did you say?"

"I'm not sure why they wanted to know your birthday, but there was something definitely up with that, so I lied and said that you were a Valentine's Day baby."

My stomach clenched. Why would she want to know when my birthday was? My knee bounced up and down. I needed to talk to Finn. Maybe I was being paranoid, but I had a feeling that Marlie-Beth knew more about me than I knew about me.

I gave Hannah a half-hug, which was hard to do because of our desks. "I'm sorry that they are bothering you, but I really appreciate you covering for me."

"That's what friends do," Hannah said. "Also, I've been thinking. You're going to think that this is crazy, but I think your power is so strong that it's allowing me to be stronger."

"What?"

"Okay, so yesterday in magic class, I actually healed a plant. You know how I come from Haniel's line, right?"

I nodded.

"She is known for her psychic abilities and healing arts. Even when I fully come into my gift, there isn't much hope for me. My power has been judged to top out at a level one, maybe a two, so the most I should be able to do in the future is have good intuition, like 'nah, dude, stay away from that pizza slice because that's a bad idea' intuition. But yesterday, I touched a leaf of a dying ivy and guess what? It became greener and healthier right in front of my eyes. Of course I couldn't tell anyone, but how cool is that?"

"Um, cool. But I don't think it has anything to do with me."

"Oh yeah? Well, tell me why I can see Remy right now, and you're not touching her?"

I looked over my shoulder to see that Remy had come into the classroom and was sitting on the teacher's desk. She was snickering while she changed the grades on the students' papers.

I looked at Hannah in shock. "How is that possible?"

"Don't know. Don't care. I'm just over here, enjoying life at the moment. Wait until I tell Remy. She's going to be so excited. We are like the only two people who can see her."

Mrs. Fields came in right then, stopping me from asking my next question.

"I apologize for being a few minutes late. Something came up that couldn't be avoided." She pulled her desk chair out and sat down.

Remy made funny faces at her as she swung her legs.

Hannah laughed, causing Remy to narrow her eyes at her. Hannah gave her a wink, and Remy's mouth flew open.

"Please take out your workbooks. You may get with your partners if you wish."

Something was off with Mrs. Fields. She was being way too chill, but I wouldn't complain.

Today, we were learning about the fifteen archangels' powers. Some of the angels had similar skills, but for the most part, each one brought something different to the table. We were to write down the angels that we came from, along with what powers they obtained. Then we were supposed to write down our level of power and what we thought we should be able to do according to the level we were on.

At the top of my paper, I listed Gabriel and Azrael since, at this point, the school still believed that I was unsure of my lineage.

My throat tightened as I looked upon Gabriel's face. She was as gorgeous as she was elegant. There was an air about her that was pure confidence. I read with interest that she could deliver messages across the veil to the dead, and Azrael, who had an uncanny resemblance to Keanu Reeves, could see the deceased, along with delivering them to the light when they were ready to go. That was pretty cool. They went hand in hand.

After writing a summary on them, I wrote what I thought I should be able to do upon my eighteenth birthday when I came into my powers.

I had time to spare, so I went through all the angels' powers, trying to retain as much as I could. After all, I had been blessed by more than a few of the archangels.

Ariel was a blonde-haired, blue-eyed hottie who could communicate with animals and nature. That explained why I could communicate with animals, and the trees did that funny thing, like trying to comfort me when I was upset. Raphael had beautiful olive skin and jet-black hair. He could heal physical wounds. Uriel was tall and skinny. His wavy, light brown hair grazed the tops of his shoulders. He shined a light on your weaknesses, helping you to overcome whatever barriers lay before you and amplified your strengths.

I cast a look over at Hannah, who was busy writing her essay. Maybe she was onto something. If I were blessed by the seven archangels, I'd have to assume that it was Uriel's gift that allowed me to help Hannah grow stronger.

I skimmed over Zadkiel, who looked like a Viking with long red hair and his long, bushy beard. Apparently, his gift was the gift of kindness and forgiveness. Definitely wasn't touched by Zadkiel. I could hold a grudge like no other.

I skipped over Haniel and went to Raziel with his dark hair, black eyes, and tanned skin. He was small in stature and extremely attractive. He was listed as the most knowledgeable of the angels, always knowing the correct answer.

Raguel almost looked dainty because of his angelic features. His blond hair and blue eyes sat in a pretty face. He was the logical one. The angel of justice.

Michael was labeled as everyone's favorite bodyguard. He was handsome with his long, brown hair and golden eyes. Strength and power were behind his smile.

Jophiel was gorgeous with her umber skin and shiny black hair that hung to her waist. Her gift was confidence and finding beauty within.

Chamuel, the one that Sandalphon had said was extremely protective of me, looked like a soldier. He stood tall and proud, well over six-foot-four, with massive shoulders. I lightly touched the image of yet another angel who had blessed me, and my heart clenched. I wish I could remember him. Below his image, it said one of his strengths was intuition. I remembered all the times I relied on my intuition to keep me safe, and I silently thanked him.

Jeremiel's skin was as dark as midnight, and his smile was as bright as the sun. How unfair to not remember that smile. He was a dream walker. Remy had been right. There was a good chance that I was a dream walker, too.

The twins were last. They both looked a little like the comic hero Thor. Metatron was a little less muscular and a few inches shorter. He gave the gift of energy.

Last, but not least, was Sandalphon. I studied his picture, seeing the commander in him. Same bone structure and physique. Sandalphon and his twin both had blond hair and blue eyes. Meanwhile, Finn had the most amazing shade of green eyes that I'd ever seen. I didn't know why this bothered me, but it did. Maybe it was because they seemed so familiar? I wondered if I had dreamed of him before.

I elbowed Hannah. "Hey, did you know that the commander comes from Sandalphon's line?"

Hannah shook her head.

"Yeah, well, he does. But does he look like him? I mean, other than the bone structure?"

"Dude, you've been memorizing the commander's bone structure?"

I rolled my eyes. "Just answer the question."

"No, he doesn't look like Sandalphon."

"Hannah, do you know who all the fully blessed at the school are?"

She tapped her chin with a finger. "Maybe. I mean, a lot of kids have been touched at some point by the archangels and or the darken."

"What's a lot?"

She shrugged. "I think there are four hundred at this school, and half of those are demis, so two hundred."

"That's a lot of power under one roof."

"Yeah, but you forget that not all of the darken are powerful, and some of the archangels were weak in power, like Haniel. That's why they give us our power level when we come in."

I sat back in my chair, thinking. Sariel had said that I didn't even have a number that could be given to me. I had a horrible feeling that I wasn't going to be able to hide who I was for much longer.

twenty-one

WHEN CLASS WAS OVER, HANNAH and I parted ways, and that was when I saw Trev leaning up against some lockers. His hands were in his pockets, and Marlie-Beth was all over him, looking like she was two seconds from ripping off his clothes. He smiled at something she said, and I couldn't help my eye roll. Was this the same boy who had tried to kiss me yesterday?

Shaking my head, I walked toward the locker rooms and changed into my training attire for hand-to-hand. I was stretching when Trev came out of the boy's locker rooms. He came over and sat right next to me.

I had to bite my cheek so that I didn't say something catty about him and Marlie-Beth. After all, it wasn't any of my business.

Remy flew into the gymnasium and plopped down right

in front of me. "Geez. This place smells like ass."

Trev started talking, but I wasn't paying attention as Remy was almost blocking Trev with her body. "Okay, so I went through all of Mrs. Fields' journals, right? By the way, I think she found the penises I drew, because the old bat had someone come ward her room. Like I would intentionally want to go back in there. It's probably the first and last time that old girl will have anyone willingly go into her room. Anyway, I checked Mr. Montgomery's room and came up with nothing but some naughty magazines. Who'd have thought he was a perv? Same thing with Mrs. Gregory. I mean, not the naughty magazine bit, but there were no books. Well, there were books on weapon training, but not books on anything to do with the academies. But baby, I got lucky in Dr. Howler's office."

I couldn't say much, so I raised my eyebrows and nodded silently, begging her to continue.

"So, here is what I found—"

"Gabriella?"

I turned to Trev. "Yes, sorry, what?"

He laughed. "I only had to say your name five times. You haven't been listening to a word I've said, have you?"

I gave him a sheepish look.

"What are you thinking about so hard?"

Remy was pissed that she had been interrupted, and the feeling was mutual.

"Sorry, I'm just tired. What do you need?" I didn't intend for that to come out impatient and bitchy, but it did.

"*Need?*" His forehead wrinkled. "I don't need anything. I just wanted to see how your day was going, that's all."

"Um, good. Well, I mean as good as any day can be here at this hellhole."

"Do you want to warm up together?"

No, not really. I wanted to hear what Remy had found.

I hesitated for a second, causing a look of confusion to come across Trev's face.

"Ugh," Remy said. "I'll never be able to tell you the scoop with this overachiever interrupting every five seconds. I'll find you at lunch."

I said to Remy, "Okay, sounds good," but it was Trev who was beaming.

"Okay, I'll go get us a couple of jump ropes."

Trev tried several times to make small talk, but I wasn't feeling it. My mind was somewhere else. Maybe Remy had found something that would answer one of the several questions that I had about the academies.

The class seemed to last forever before Mr. Montgomery finally dismissed us.

I changed clothes as quickly as I could and was exiting the locker room at the same time as Trev. I put my head down as I barreled past him so I wouldn't get stuck talking. Hopefully, he didn't see me. I needed to get to lunch quickly. I knew my ghost would come through for me.

twenty-two

USUALLY, LUNCHTIME WAS MY FAVORITE because I could sit and relax under my tree with the mountains as my backdrop, but I was too anxious to relax today. After I got my tray, I debated whether to eat inside where there was a ton of kids or sit outside and take the risk of getting ambushed by the crew.

The hell with them. I refused to let them take my favorite place from me. Plus, it would be easier to communicate with Remy.

I arrived at what I had deemed my tree to see Finn sitting there with a book in his lap.

"Wh-what are you doing?" I stuttered.

Without looking up, he said, "It looks like I'm reading. What are you doing?"

"Sorry, that was rude. I just meant that I've kind of

started to think of this as my spot, so it just surprised me to see someone else sitting under it. Especially you."

Finally looking up at me, he said, "Well, it is a big tree. I think two can fit under it."

Well, great. Remy was supposed to be meeting here, and now all she would be thinking of was the commander's nice ass. I didn't know why my best friend was so focused on that one part. I mean, it was great, but there were other excellent parts, too.

While he flipped a page in his book, my gaze traveled up his muscular thighs stretched out before him and up to his torso that had to be magnificent under that cotton shirt. I mean, everything else on him was fan-flipping-tastic, so why wouldn't his abs be, as well? My eyes roamed over his bulging biceps. I felt myself getting hot as I made my way up to study his profile.

Finn coughed uncomfortably. His jaw was clenched, and he was squeezing the book he had in his hand so hard that the pages were almost ripping from the spine.

"Are you okay?" I asked.

He slowly turned his head to look at me. "You find me attractive?"

Um ... What the hell kind out of the blue question was that?

"It was a question I would like an answer to."

I narrowed my eyes. I had asked once before if he could read my mind, and he replied I was just easy to read.

Feeling confident in that, I said, "I have no clue why you

would ask such a question."

One corner of his mouth lifted as he gave me a knowing smile. "That's fair."

I scanned the courtyard for Remy. The commander was acting super strange, and my friend couldn't show up a moment too soon.

Finn chuckled. "Are you wanting out of my presence?"

I swiveled my head back toward him. His green eyes started twinkling with amusement. A girl could get lost in those for days.

"I've always hated the color of my eyes."

"Um, I'm sorry?"

"Maybe I can readjust my thinking if you're that enamored with them."

I pushed my tray off my lap, scooting back as far as I could until I felt the bark eating into my back. *Did he just hear my thoughts?* I quickly went through all the archangels' powers. I was damned sure that mindreading wasn't a gift of any of theirs. So, how in the world had he known my thoughts?

Finn leaned in close to me, whispering, "That's a good question. Which is why I'm here today. Any more dreams?"

I was freaking mortified. He was *so* reading my mind.

I was pissed as I quickly started going through all the things I had thought about when it concerned Finn to see if I should be embarrassed. I had just analyzed every glorious inch of him, and I was pretty sure that would classify as embarrassing.

I barely bit back a groan at the arrogant smile on the commander's face.

"Dreams?" he prompted.

"Yeah, I saw Camaella crying in all her shame, and I saw my wedding day."

He sat up straighter. His brows came together as he leaned into me. "Say that one more time."

My head fell back against the bark of the tree. "Apparently, I was married at some point. I dreamed of the day my mother, Gabriel, helped me get dressed. Then the dream faded into Camaella crying on the floor."

"That's all you saw?" He sounded almost disappointed.

"Yep. I keep thinking: what if I left a whole family behind when I died?"

We sat there in silence for a few minutes, with me wondering about who I left behind and Finn frowning over who knew what.

I finally broke the silence. "Can you at least tell me if you hear my thoughts all the time?"

Finn hesitated, looking as if he was taking a moment to weigh his words. Finally, he pointed up to the leaves above us. They were blowing so hard on the branches that they looked like they were shaking. "Would you say this happens when you're agitated or stressed?"

I nodded.

"Then, when those emotions come to you, you're at your weakest, and it's easy for me to pick up on what you're not saying."

"So, just when I'm agitated?"

He gave me a nod.

"Well, that's not saying much because, since I've been at this place, I've been stressed and agitated."

He laughed as he closed his book. "You can keep me from your thoughts. I almost hate to tell you how, though."

I gave him the stank eye. "Spill it."

"Build a wall in your mind; make it as high as it will go. Then I won't be privy to your thoughts." He pulled a long leg in and propped an elbow on it. "There are four weeks until your birthday on New Year's Day. I want you to be prepared as much as possible, but I just don't know if there is enough time."

"Because …?"

His green eyes flashed to mine. "Because—" Without taking his eyes off me, he said, "Your friend is here."

"You can see Remy, too?"

He shook his head. "No, your other friend." He looked at my lips, causing my heart to skip a beat. "I'll just take my magnificent physique somewhere else."

That was it. I was going to officially die of embarrassment.

Finn was chuckling as, out of the corner of my eye, I saw Trev walking up to where we were sitting, but I couldn't take my eyes off Finn.

Finn stood up, almost towering over Trev. Both guys stared at one another for what seemed like forever before Finn gave me one last look then walked around Trev.

After a couple of moments of silence, Trev decided to take a seat next to me, right where Finn had been sitting.

His handsome face looked harder now, like he was clearly upset but fighting hard to conceal it. "I could see the intensity in that conversation from a mile away. Want to tell me what it was about?"

He wanted me to tell him about a private conversation I had been having? Why would it be any of his business?

Seeing Marlie-Beth fawn all over him might have made me a tad pissed with Trev.

I shrugged. "Oh, nothing in particular." *Just the commander calling me out on my private thoughts. Damn him.*

He narrowed his eyes, and I thought for a second that he was going to call me on my B.S., but then he just put his hands on his knees and said, "Okay, cool. Just checking to make sure you were all right. I wanted to see if you'd like to join me for lunch, but I forgot I had to do something, so I'll just catch you later."

I picked up my tray from the grass and said, "Sure. Later."

Before he walked away, Trev said, "Be careful who you trust, beautiful."

One could only assume he was talking about the commander.

His words weighed heavily on me. The commander had been telling me not to trust anyone, too. Maybe he was also including himself.

I believed that Finn was truly trying to protect me, but I guessed I could just be a secret weapon for him to use further on down the line. I needed to keep my guard up.

Once again, I scanned the courtyard. Where the hell was Remy? I needed company and dreaded eating the rest of my lunch in solitude.

Since Remy looked like a no-show, I picked up my tray and went to find Hannah. I knew exactly where she would be—outside of the library with her nose stuck in a book.

Magic class with Dr. Howler was always a bore for me as I sat beside Hannah, pretending not to have any gifts. If I let on that I could do half the things I could, then everyone would connect the dots and know I wasn't just the demi I was pretending to be. But you'd think that I would need to get better at the gifts I currently wielded. How was I supposed to prepare for a battle against the darken if I didn't practice? I was beyond frustrated, and my agitation was making Hannah's plant leaves lean toward me.

She kicked me under the table. "Cut it out, will you? Someone might notice."

Just about that time, the commander came busting through the door. I watched as his eyes roamed the classroom, stopping when he saw me.

"Dr. Howler, I need to see Gabriella for a moment."

All the kids snickered as I made my way out to the

hallway, gently closing the door behind me.

"Are you all right?" he asked.

"Yeah, why?"

He folded his arms over his chest. "I was next door, observing Mrs. Fields' class. She swears that one of the students is changing the class grades. By the way, you wouldn't know anything about that, would you?"

"Nope."

He narrowed his eyes but let it go. "Anyway, I could hear your thoughts from the next room."

Note to self: get better at building walls.

The thought that I was being that loud was upsetting.

"First off, do grades really count here? I mean, I know that there is something awful coming my way and soon. I feel it. I seriously doubt the grades are going to count. Maybe we do need the knowledge, and maybe we need the training, but seriously? Grades?"

A smile stretched over his face as he rocked back on his heels. "Actually, yes, grades do count. Failing in there means that you could fail outside of the academy when you go up against a demon or, worse, a darken. Now, you want to tell me what's wrong?"

"Okay, maybe I am frustrated. I'm sitting in that class, but I'm not allowed to participate because, if I do, I might accidentally show my hand, and everyone will know that I'm not just a demi, but you say I have to get stronger. You see the dilemma?"

He let out a sigh. "I do. So, what if, during this time, I

meet you at the cabin to train?"

His cabin twice in a day?

"What about the library? It's right across the hall. And is there any way that Hannah could also come?" I felt my cheeks flushing as I rushed to explain, "The kids were snickering when you called me out here, and then I'm already meeting you for additional training once a day." Lord, I was blushing. "You know, kids talk."

He took a step toward me, closing in on me, and I tilted my chin up to look at him. My body was reacting to him in a way that I would die of mortification if he knew what I was thinking. Unfortunately, I hadn't nailed the whole building a wall inside my mind thing yet, so instead of thinking of how badly I wanted him to dip his head and kiss me, I made myself think of puppies. They were cute and cuddly, and everyone loved puppies.

A grin split his face. "Puppies? When we first met, it was tacos and unicorns, and now it's puppies?" He reached out, lightly skimming my face with a finger, before he pushed a strand of hair behind my ear. "Let me grab Hannah, and we will go to the library for this class."

I felt like banging my head into the wall as he walked away. I would learn how to build walls tonight. That was a high priority.

After Dr. Howler excused a very curious Hannah, we all headed to the library, where I explained to her that this would be our new magic class. She was trying to pretend like the commander training her was no big deal, but the uncontrollable, nervous laugh that she was releasing at the end of all her sentences gave her away. The commander simply smiled at her patiently.

I couldn't blame her. He just had this way about him that commanded everyone to stop what they were doing and take notice of him. It wasn't just because he was handsome. Part of it was the masculinity rolling off him in waves.

He locked the three of us in the library with a closed sign for privacy. Then we sat at one of the round tables with Finn between Hannah and me. He reminded us that neither one of us was eighteen yet, so until our gifts came out to play, we wouldn't be at our full potential, so he would not judge us on how badly we did during the hour.

He handed Hannah a book and told her to close her eyes and concentrate. He wanted to see if she could understand what the subject matter would be without opening the book. When she hesitated, Finn reassured her that he didn't expect much. All he was asking was for a feeling about what the book could possibly be about.

Trying hard to impress him, she sat as still as a statue, eyes closed, sporting a funny, strained expression.

He turned to me and whispered, "You're a different story. You have already been demonstrating some significant powers. I've seen Azrael's power in you when you communicate with Remy. With your dreams, you're using Jeremiel's gift. The plants and trees are Ariel's hand. Your great intuition is Chamuel's calling card." He handed me a book. "But what about Haniel's gift of psychic abilities? Can you do the same thing as your friend Hannah?"

I grabbed the book and tried not to wiggle in my seat. I had never asked to see Remy or communicate with animals; it just came naturally. This was a whole new world to me.

I sat there for what felt like an eternity. I stopped thinking about what I was supposed to do and just freed my mind. The book trembled slightly in my hands.

"The book is about the plague that wiped out most of the humans back in 520 AD. Supposedly, 10,000 people died a day."

I opened my eyes to the sound of clapping. Finn was smiling from ear to ear. "Fantastic."

Hannah narrowed her eyes. "I thought you were touched by Gabriel and Azrael. No one said anything about Haniel."

Feeling horrible for lying to my best friend, I gave Finn a pleading look.

He turned to Hannah. "This goes against my better judgment, but in the future, Gabriella might need you, so you should know the truth. Gabriella was touched by a few of the archangels."

Hannah crossed her lanky arms over her chest and looked from the commander to me. "How many exactly is a few?"

"I just used Haniel's gifts, so I guess the count is officially eight," I said.

"*Eight?*" she shouted. "Are you freaking kidding me

right now? Why wouldn't you tell me?"

I pointed at Finn. "Because he basically said it was life or death."

Finn clenched his jaw. "Just so that we are all clear, it still is. I assume you ladies will catch Remy up on everything, but not another soul is to know this information. Understood?" He barked the last part, making Hannah sit up taller.

We both said, "Yes," at the same time.

"So, were you lying when you said you weren't touched by a darken?"

I shook my head, causing her eyes to widen.

"So the strongest person here at the academy is truly a demi?"

"Technically, she's not a demi." Finn said. "But, for her safety, that's what we're going with."

I had already decided to wait until we were alone to tell her who my mother was. I had a feeling she was going to freak when she found out I was Nephilim.

Hannah snorted before she scooted back from the table with a huff. "Okay, big guy, switch seats with me."

A very confused Finn stood, so Hannah could sit next to me. She held her book with one hand, and with the other, she grabbed my wrist. "Okay, girlfriend, share some of that juice with me."

After a couple of minutes, Hannah smirked as she threw her book on the table. "My book is about all the fallen angels and the reason they fell. *Boom!* That just happened."

"Amazing," Finn said. "You can assist in her gift."

I nodded. "We came across that when I was touching Remy, and she was able to see her."

"But that's not the best part," Hannah said. "I can see her now without Gabriella touching her, too."

Finn leaned back in his chair, placing both hands behind his neck. His T-shirt was stretched taut over his torso, and I was pretty sure Hannah had stopped breathing. "No one has known exactly how powerful you would be, Gabriella, but power-sharing? That's almost unfathomable. I'd like for you to call upon Azrael's power, and then summon Remy."

"Summon? Yeah, I don't think that's going to work."

"Of course it will. It's like placing a call without a phone," he said.

He didn't understand. Even if I could summon Remy, it wasn't a great idea. You didn't summon a queen. She was going to kill me.

I closed my eyes and tried to mentally call her. I felt so silly sitting there with my brow furrowed as I telepathically called Remy's name over and over.

Right when I was about to give up, I saw a pissed off Remy gliding toward me at a fast pace.

"No, you did *not* just drag me here." Her blue eyes flashed to me. "I'm not a dog, you know."

I threw my hands up in the air. "So not my fault. I knew you'd be pissed off." I pointed at Finn. "He made me."

"Um, why?"

"As you probably noticed, Hannah could see you this

morning in Mrs. Fields' class. We told the commander about it, and now he's curious."

Remy made a chair scoot back before she plopped into it. "Can you see me, Hannah?"

"Yes, and hear you, too!" she squealed. "Isn't this so exciting?"

I smiled at her happiness. "Apparently, it's called power-sharing. No one else at school saw you, or they would have been talking about it. I think, with this gift, it's like I'm giving permission for certain people to see you. Can the commander see you?"

She swept her bangs to the side as she rolled her eyes. "I don't know. I mean, I like playing pranks, and if he can see me—"

"Say no more." I leveled a look at Finn. "If I let you see her, and she does anything remotely inappropriate, which she will because that's how she rolls, you have to ignore it. She's a ghost and has very little enjoyment left."

Remy said, "Geez, woman. It's not that depressing," as Finn said, "Understood."

Remy placed her hand in mine, and we watched as Finn smiled slowly. Remy returned the smile. I should have realized how lonely Remy had been.

"Hey, Remy, nice to see you again," Finn said.

"Commander, it is always a pleasure to see you."

The way she said it was sensual, causing the commander to squirm in his seat and me and Hannah to laugh.

"This is very hopeful, Gabriella," Finn said.

Remy looked at her nails. "Nancy Drew here is kinda in the middle of some things. I gotta go. We will catch up later?"

I gave her a nod.

"And don't be yanking my string again unless someone is about to murder you."

After she left, we went back to practicing Haniel's gift. I was only half paying attention, too busy thinking of what Remy was in the middle of.

Eventually, Hannah said she could do no more. Her head was pounding from the effort of using her gift.

The commander dismissed us, and I headed off to cardio training. Maybe I would never be able to fight off a couple of demons, but if I was lucky enough, I could outrun them.

twenty-three

MY PRIVATE LESSONS WITH THE commander were a success. I was getting better and better at hand-to-hand. He refused to pull his punches, but thanks to my angel-blessed healing abilities, I usually only sported bruises for half a day or so.

We were both quiet as we left his cabin. When he stopped walking, I gave a little wave goodbye to him, and then Finn watched me pass through the courtyard as I headed back to my dorm. He had wanted to walk me all the way to my room, but I'd begged him not to. The kids were already snickering about me. It was enough that I could still feel his eyes on me as I walked.

I sighed as I neared my building. The thought of climbing those steps to my room made me want to cry. The workout he had put me through had been vigorous,

and I was sore. Plus, I was mentally exhausted from all the reading I'd been doing. Finn had tons of interesting books that I was hoping would somehow help me in the future. So far, I hadn't learned anything awe-inspiring when it came to battling demons.

I heard footsteps pounding on the sidewalk. Someone was trying to catch up to me. My heart rate picked up, and I began to panic.

I looked over my shoulder to see a smiling Trev.

"Hey, I was hoping I would see you. Can we talk?"

"Sure. What's up?"

"Why are you mad at me?"

"Why would you think I'm mad?"

A group of students went around us as they headed inside the dormitory. One of them was Marlie-Beth.

I jerked my head in her direction. "So, you and her are a thing now, huh?"

"What?" He gave a sexy smile. "No, we're not, and we will never be. This wouldn't have anything to do with why you've been standoffish to me recently, would it?"

"What?"

"The other day, I saw you pass us in the hall when she was trying to talk with me. I tried to catch up with you, but you were already in the girls' locker room, and then, right after that, you practically ignored me during hand-to-hand training."

"Um ..." I couldn't say *no, I was talking to my dead bestie*. "I've just been drained and consumed here lately.

I'm not upset with you, I promise."

His eyebrows rose while he nodded. He obviously didn't believe a word I had just said. If I kept insisting I wasn't angry, it would only get awkward, but considering his spirits seemed to have lifted dramatically, I let it go.

I casually looked behind me to see the commander. From this distance, I couldn't see his face, but his body language was an entirely different manner. He really hated Trev.

Hannah was crossing the courtyard from a different direction. Some of the boys had played a game of cricket behind the school, and while I was training with Finn, she had gone to watch them. She wanted to see if she could put her psychic abilities to the test now that I'd given her a boost. I waved her over. Maybe she could ease some of this weirdness going on between Trev and me.

I looked one more time to where Finn was, and Trev caught my glance.

"I heard that you had another private lesson with the commander today during magic class."

I shook my head. "It wasn't private. There was another student with me." I didn't mention that it was Hannah, and only because I requested her to be in there.

Hannah came to stand beside me as Trev asked, "Why is he giving you special treatment in magic, though?"

I felt forced to lie, and it didn't sit well with me. "Because I'm a demi who's uncertain of my lineage, which is unheard of, so he is monitoring my power."

Hannah nodded. "I hear that he quietly helps other

students, as well." Man, she could lie so much better than me. "He's actually helping me, too, because I am the lowest leveled fully blessed at the academy. I mean, Gabriella is a demi, and she is probably more powerful than me."

Trev seemed to like our answers.

"Hey, so this weekend, they are showing a movie outdoors. Tomorrow night, actually, in the quad; you want to go?" He looked at Hannah. "You, too, Hannah. It'll be fun."

I looked at my friend, who gave me a shrug. "All right. What time is it showing?"

"Nine."

"Okay," I said. "See you then."

"It's a date," he said.

He looked happy as he jogged off in the opposite direction than me and Hannah were heading.

"He's got it bad for you," she said. "I almost feel bad for him."

"Should I take offense?"

"No, I meant that the commander also likes you. And in the real world, Trev would be the top of the food chain, but this isn't the real world. This is the world where angels have been blessing people, and they blessed the commander as the top of the food chain. The man is smoking hot. Either way, you'll have to turn one of them down at some point, and that is going to be crushing for their ego. Neither one of them have probably ever heard the word *no* before."

"Wait—back it up. Why would you say that about the

commander?"

"Don't look now, but he's been boring a hole into your head."

"He hates Trev."

"Maybe. But he also hates that you talk to Trev." She threw a long arm over my shoulders, ushering me into the building.

It took all my will power not to look back at Finn.

"So, I went to watch the boys play a game of croquet, and I picked up on their thoughts. I mean, it was staticky, but I heard some."

"Well, that's going to be a neat trick to have."

"Yeah, it won't help when we are in a fight to the death with some demon, but it'll be a good party trick."

I laughed. She did have a point.

As we walked toward my room, she said, "I don't know about you, but I have this sense of dread. Like, soon, everything is going to change, but for the worst."

I knew exactly what she was saying. I felt like there was a big, black cloud hanging over my head.

twenty-four

MY DREAMS BLISSFULLY CAME TO me quickly that night. I dreamed of an angel who had eyes so vibrant that surely poems had been written about them. He was so beautiful that I wanted—no, I needed—to get closer. I watched him as he went down a narrow hall and down a spiraling staircase. He moved with such confidence and grace that it almost looked like he floated above the ground.

At the bottom of the stairs, he walked past several doors. There were screams and moans coming from behind them. His beautiful smile intensified upon hearing their cries. Finally, he went to the door that held what he was looking for. He waved a hand in front of the knob, and the door lock was magically released.

Camaella sat on the floor, weeping. Her head was on the floor, her back exposed. It was raw and bleeding from where her wings had been torn from her.

As soon as she saw the beautiful angel, she whimpered and tried to crawl into a corner. She had loved him, lost her wings for him, and he had betrayed her. He didn't have feelings for her. He had just been using her the entire time.

The angel tsked. "Now, vixen, why would you run from me? After all, I thought we were friends." He squatted down to be on her level. His stunning eyes flickered with amusement. "I've come to make you a deal, one that you might actually enjoy this time." When Camaella didn't utter a word, he continued, "I've decided to release you from hell. You are free to roam the earth as a civilian, or you can work as my commander. The choice is yours."

"Why …? Why would you do that?"

"What? Release you, or offer you a job as my commander?"

Her forehead scrunched, looking like she was trying to figure out what trap Lucifer had laid for her. "Either."

He gave a casual shrug. "Hell is my domain. It is where I must stay, but I need eyes and ears above. Besides, I thought you might enjoy having the power that only I can give you. Plus, you can watch the archangels perish under your hand."

Camaella sniffled. "How?"

He snapped his fingers. "Oh, that's right. You've been locked down here. It's a shame that things ran its course with us, but you know what they say: all mediocre things must come to an end. Would you like me to share with you what I was doing when I visited earth?"

She gave a stiff nod.

"Then, after that, you can tell me what your decision is. You can take on earth as a human or become my commander." He rubbed his hands together, as if he was gearing up to tell a good story. Then he stood up and dusted his palms.

"I have found the Flaming Sword."

"What?" Camaella exclaimed.

His smile widened. *"I know. So fascinating. It has been right under our noses this whole entire time. Azrael has had it in plain sight."* He chuckled. *"Cheeky bugger. He always was ballsy.*

"I need that sword, Camaella." Frustration coated his tone. *"For years, my intel has told me that the archangels are flocking to one place. At first, I thought it was because they were super needy, but now I think it might be because of something more.*

"There is a wedding that will take place tomorrow. I want you there. As my commander, it would be your job to wield the blade against the archangels. Kill as many as possible."

"Kill them?" Her voice was hoarse from all the screaming she had been doing.

"Yes, poppet." He gave her a disdainful look. *"What else would we do with them?"* He sighed deeply as he pinched the bridge of his nose. *"You know what? Maybe you aren't the right choice for the job."*

He started to leave, but she called out to him, *"Wait! Of course I can kill the archangels. I can do this."*

Lucifer hid his grin as he turned around. *"So, you agree to be bound to me, to carry my mark, and be my loyal servant?"*

"Yes," she said.

"Good. There is only one being there you cannot kill. All else is fair game."

"Who am I to not touch?"

"My son, of course." He gave her a wink. "Trust me; you'll recognize him when you see him. A chip off the old block, that one is."

She was hesitant before she asked the question that was burning in the back of her mind. "Will Sandalphon be there?"

Lucifer rolled his eyes and gave an exaggerated sigh. "Oh, poppet, please tell me you are not still carrying a torch for that pompous archangel."

"No, of course not. It's just that he is mighty."

"Worry not, love. I'm sending in an army of demons to distract everyone. Besides, you'd need to worry more over my son's strength than Sandalphon. I fear the archangels have brainwashed him. That was a plan that backfired on me. Nonetheless, hopefully, we will be able to call to his darker side tomorrow. We could really use him in the future." He rubbed a hand across his square jaw. "The archangels are making demis, and if we can bless the demis, as well, then, when the war comes, they will hear my call and hopefully join forces with us. All I'm doing is evening out the battlefield, love."

She nodded. "And once we have the blessed on our side?"

"We will rule earth, and I will be freed from hell." He walked over to her and lightly stroked her face. "You'd be my queen," the Prince of Lies said seductively.

Determination shone in her eyes. Whether it was due to the power he dangled over her head or if it was because she craved to be back in his arms, he wasn't sure, but his job was done. He had broken Camaella, and the broken ones were always the ones who had more to prove when they finally made their way back to their feet. He had no doubt that Camaella would be the perfect commander for his growing army.

Camaella slowly stood, her body so broken that it hurt to breathe. "If I agree to become your commander, am I free to go?"

"Yes, but before you do, have one of the servants clean you up. You look like you've been in hell. And don't forget to report back to me every so often."

I woke up drenched in sweat. The devil was in the details, and I was missing some pretty important ones. Like, was that *my* damn wedding they had crashed? How did he know that there had been a wedding taking place? I might not remember my past life, but I was pretty damn sure that I didn't send out an invite to the Prince of Darkness.

twenty-five

WEEKENDS AT THE ACADEMY WERE like everything else at the school—they sucked. Saturdays, we still had to do our magic class and hand-to-hand combat training. Then, after those two classes, all the first year demis and the fully blessed were encouraged to go to the training field to watch the demis fight against each other. Some of the sophomores were clumsy, but for the most part, all of them flowed like skilled warriors.

Trev was sitting with a group of kids, and when he saw me, he gave me a wave with one of his charming smiles.

Hannah nudged my leg. "Hey, look, the demis are done warming up. Now they are going to have some fun." She wiggled her orange eyebrows. "I hope the boys take off their shirts. I need some excitement in my life."

I laughed at my crazy friend as the demis broke off into

four teams, leaving them with under fifty demis in each group. Then the first two groups fought each other with a weapon that looked like a wooden staff, with a tip coated in red paint. Once the red paint got anywhere on your person, you were out.

Hannah was cheering for the second-year students who were battling the seniors. They didn't look like they stood a chance. Not just because of their size, but they had less training, and it showed in the way they moved.

The commander stood on the sidelines. It was hard keeping my attention on the game when his presence was so domineering. His muscular thighs were parted, and his arms were braced across his chest. His expression gave away nothing. Fierce and hot. I felt safe with my assessment of him because I thought I had finally figured out how to build my walls. The more I practiced, the easier the mental wall formed.

Every once and a while, he would congratulate someone on the field or bark a constructive comment to a demi who had gotten outplayed.

In the end, the second-year students got brutally slaughtered.

Before the start of the next game, Remy joined us on the bleachers. Hannah was having a hard time talking to Remy without it looking like she was talking to thin air, so I had to keep elbowing her.

Exasperated, she said, "Sorry. So, Remy, what did you find out from Dr. Howler's private chambers?"

"Some interesting shit, that's what," she said.

"Are you going to tell us, or do you need a drumroll, princess?" I asked.

"Bitch mode initiated." She looked at her nails. "You *so* don't deserve to hear this juicy intel, but I'm going to share with you both from the goodness of my heart." She paused before announcing, "Our commander knows where the object is that could help us win the war."

Hannah asked, "Come again?"

"You heard me, bitches. Apparently, the one thing that could save us all from the darken and their nasty little demons is this blade called the Flaming Sword. The commander supposedly knows where it is, but he won't tell. Dr. Howler's journal said that the commander was hired by the Empowered Academy as a ruse, and when he wouldn't tell his colleagues where it was, they brought in a whole squad to torture him for the info. He escaped and built this place as another option for the demis and blessed."

"Not going to lie," Remy said, "but the Empowered Academy sounds like a bag of dicks."

I nodded. "Yeah."

I wanted to tell my best friends that I also knew where the Flaming Sword was, but I had a feeling that Finn would flip the hell out, so I kept my mouth shut.

If I made it out of here alive, there would be a lot of people after me. Demons, darken, and most likely the Empowered Academy. It was just a matter of time before everyone knew that I was more than I was pretending to be.

I watched the commander across the field. I needed to do the binding ritual with him. The only thing holding me back was him knowing all my emotions, and I wasn't sure if I could build a wall high enough to keep him out of my thoughts. Regardless, there was no one better to protect me. I needed to go through with it. The sooner, the better.

The three of us watched the next game in silence. By the next match, Remy and Hannah had quit frowning, and by the third and final game, I was cheering just as loudly as Hannah. Remy thought we were nerds, but my heart felt lighter when we left the stadium. After the dream I'd had last night, I needed something less stressful in my life. A little normalcy went a long way.

Remy said her goodbyes as soon as she saw the crew. She wanted to go terrorize them while she still had the energy. Bless her sweet ghostly heart.

Hannah wanted to go get some food, and I had my own agenda.

The commander was walking across the field with several students when I caught his eye as I made my way down the bleachers and jerked my head toward the locker rooms. He gave me a brief nod before patting a student on the back.

I waited patiently for him to finish talking with a few of the demis and greeted some students as they made their way to the locker room.

That familiar tug had me turning around to see the commander quickly approaching.

With those green eyes, he scanned me quickly. "What's wrong?"

"Nothing. I just wanted to talk to you about a couple of things."

He crossed his muscular arms over his chest. "I'm listening."

"First, I want to do the binding. I've thought about it, and if it will keep me safe, I'm all for it. Second, I don't like lying to my friends. I want to tell them about me being the Flaming Sword."

He shook his head. "Absolutely not."

I took a step closer to him. "I'm not asking for permission."

He started to say something when a student walked by. Grabbing my elbow, he tugged me to the end of the hall. "The more people who know, the more danger you will be in."

"That's why I've agreed to do the binding spell."

He ran a hand through his midnight hair and bit his lip, making me clench my legs together. Thank the heavens I had my walls in place. This crush wasn't good for either of us.

"I'm not happy with this," he said. "Just to be clear, we are talking about Hannah and Remy, correct?"

I nodded. "And no one else."

"Richard is at the end of the field. Grab him and meet me at my cabin. I have a few things I have to tidy up here, and then we can do the binding spell."

"I really don't need an escort."

"Yes, you do. I found out who was behind the attempt to harm you. Devon."

My eyes widened. "Marlie-Beth and Angelina's friend, Devon?"

He clenched his jaw. "Oh, I'm sure he wasn't acting alone. I just need to prove it. When I went to his dorm this morning, he was missing, so until I find him, I don't want you by yourself."

I gave him a nod.

Nervous energy ran through me as I watched him turn on his heel, heading back toward the field.

I looked the whole field over for Richard or even Dan and came up empty. Then I glanced over at Trev. I could ask him, but then again, I didn't really want to see the judgment in his eyes. I also didn't want to wait around. Decision made I cut around the back of the athletic field and took the quiet path at a brisk pace. I almost didn't notice Devon until I was upon him.

My heart began to race. Shit.

Trying to act like I wasn't scared, I said, "Why weren't you out on the field today?"

"I had other things to do." A sleazy grin came upon his face. "So, you noticed that I wasn't playing?"

"No, I didn't notice. However, seeing as you are in regular clothes, unlike the players who were not and were still on the field when I left, I assumed you didn't play, and it looks as if I was correct."

He took a couple of strides toward me, and my heart started racing even faster. I was mentally screaming until he grabbed me roughly by the arm and tried to drag me off the path, and then there was nothing mental about the blood-curling scream I let out.

The trees began to billow back and forth as he tightened his hand around me, pushing me back up against one of the trees, the bark biting into my sensitive skin.

"You shouldn't be here," he said, bringing his hand up and around my throat, beginning to squeeze.

My vision blurred. All the combat training that I'd had went out the window as I stood there frozen.

I heard the growl before I saw the wolf. Devon slightly turned his head, giving the wolf the opening he needed as the wolf leapt at Devon's throat. The boy was quickly taken down to the ground where he thrashed in pain as he tried to get out of the wolf's strong hold, but what he didn't know was the wolf had heard my pleas and had come to save me.

Behind me, feet pounded on the ground. Finn and the Rocks, who I'd come to like, even if they did push us too hard in cardio class, were barreling toward us. I stood in shock off to the side, just watching the wolf maul Devon.

Finn shouted a command at the wolf, "Come."

The wolf hesitated for a second longer before releasing Devon with a whine. He scrambled off the boy and went to sit next to the commander.

Finn's eyes were narrow slits. "What happened?"

"It looks like I found Devon for you." I pulled my eyes away from Devon, who was holding his bloody face and crying. "I was on my way to your cabin, and he was blocking my path." My voice was scratchy from being strangled. "He mentioned that I shouldn't be here, and then he forced me off the path where he began to choke me. Then the wolf showed up." I had thought I had somehow called the wolf, but with the way the wolf was rubbing his face on the commander's pant leg, I no longer knew. Maybe I'd been mistaken.

The commander's face was nothing but masked rage as he leaned down and whispered something into Devon's ear, which momentarily made the boy stop his crying. Then the commander roughly jerked Devon up by his shirt, reared his arm back, and punched Devon so hard in the face that I heard the bone crack. The boy immediately slumped, and Finn let him fall on the hard ground in a heap.

He turned toward the Rocks. "He is to leave the academy within the hour. He is not to talk to a soul before his departure. His memory needs to be wiped of the potential location of the academy. When you drop him off at his parents' house, make sure he has left the academy in disgrace and shame. He will not graduate, and their house will not bear the mark of the demi symbol. If they give you any grief, you let me know, and I will personally pay them a visit."

Dan and Richard roughly grabbed the limp Devon from off the ground, and then I watched, still in shock, as they dragged him down the trail.

I glanced over at Finn, who was barely containing his rage. His fists were balled, and his chest was rising and falling quickly. The wolf whimpered and pawed at Finn's leg.

"What part of you need an escort did you not understand?"

I winced. "I'm sorry."

He began to pace up and down the narrow trail. Finally, he came to a stop right in front of me. "I need you to be safe."

I gave him a nod. I really was sorry. It was stupid of me. I should have just waited for him to finish up.

He didn't say anything more as he bent down to ruffle the wolf's fur.

"I thought I had called him with Ariel's gift, but I guess I was wrong. I didn't know he was a pet. He must've just heard my screams and decided to help me."

"No, you did call him, and he did used to be wild, but I rescued him and his siblings. They roam the grounds, keeping an eye out for me."

"Can …? Can you communicate with them?"

"Well, that would mean that I come from Ariel's line, and you already know which line I come from."

"Yeah, that wouldn't make sense, would it?" But as I continued to watch the wolf with Finn, I couldn't shake the feeling that they were communicating. In fact, I was almost certain Finn was talking to the wolf now.

He scanned my body for any signs of damage. "You've stopped shaking. Are you okay now?"

"Okay-ish," I rasped, tears clouding my vision. "I panicked. I didn't even try to get out of his hold. I just stood there like I was ready to die."

He wrapped his warm arms around me, cradling my head to his chest. "Yeah, you panicked. We will train more, and you'll learn not to panic." I felt his lips touch the top of my head ever so lightly.

I clung to his shirt, breathing in his scent. Even his woodsy, cedar scent reeked of masculinity. My head spun as I pulled back from him.

He wiped my tears with the pads of his thumbs then tilted my head up so I would meet his eyes and said, "I need you to tell me that you're okay."

I nodded. "I'm okay."

His emotions were making the wolf whine. He took a deep breath, his muscular chest rising with the action. "Do you still want to do the binding today?"

"Now more than ever."

Without another word, he clasped my small hand in his, and then we started walking toward his cabin with the wolf trailing beside us.

The wolf was on my heels as I entered Finn's house.

He patted the wolf on the head. "From now on, he will follow you everywhere you go."

"Everywhere? Like he will escort me home or—"

"Not just escort you, but he will be staying with you and

Remy in your dorm. He will sleep there, eat with you, and I might even make him shower with you."

I put my hands on my hips and gave him my best *are you serious?* look.

"Okay, maybe not that last one, but I can promise you that, from here on out, he will be your shadow when I'm not around."

I thought about the wolf saving me from Devon and agreed wholeheartedly. I didn't mind a shadow if it kept me safe from people like Devon.

"What happens when a demi is touched by a powerful darken?"

He stopped at my words.

"Makes them corrupt? Makes them tempted to join Lucifer's cause? How could Devon be so vile and evil, yet Hannah be so pure of heart?" I stared hard at the male in front of me. "Does it have to do with how strong the darken was that touched them?"

Knowing what I was getting at, a smile appeared on his full lips. "That's a lot of questions. And I don't think it is necessarily the strength of the angel who touches the human, but the strength of the human who has been blessed. I'm sure some would disagree, but I think that everyone has the choice to be good or bad. Maybe the odds are against you if you've been touched by a powerful darken, but at the end of the day, we all still have a choice to be who we want to be.

"Understand that Lucifer wants the fully blessed to be

on his side. He wants them to fight against the remaining archangels, and he will do whatever he can to sway them. Some of the fully blessed who have been touched by the darken won't be strong enough to resist his dark calling. They will join him and his army." He ran a hand over his stubble. "Gabriella, just remember that anyone has the potential to be good or bad. No matter who they are born from or who has touched them."

"Do you like being immortal?"

He pulled me over to the couch. "It's not all that it's cracked up to be."

I rolled my eyes. "Only you would think being immortal is a bad thing."

"It is if you have ever lost someone important."

I searched his eyes. Who had this man lost?

"In order to do the binding"—his words brought me out of my thoughts—"I'll need you close to me, and I'll need you to concentrate in order for this work. Do you understand?"

"Yes. Have you done this before?"

"No." He grabbed my hips and lifted me, setting me down on his lap. My eyes widened in surprise, and he gave me a sexy smirk. "Concentrate."

Oh sure, like that's totally possible while sitting on his lap!

I took a deep breath and closed my eyes, feeling him wrap his arms around my waist while he chanted some foreign language. I let the words slide over me.

"Let down your walls," he said. "Open yourself

completely to me."

I did as he asked, shifting on his lap as he reached for something on the coffee table. I peeked an eye open to see him grabbing a small dagger while he rubbed my back comfortingly with his free hand.

"Gabriella, we have to mix our blood while I finish out the last words. Even without your full powers, you will heal quickly, and I can also help take the pain away."

My eyes unconsciously darted to the blade then back to him. "I'm pretty damn sure that you were communicating with the wolf, you can read my mind when in close proximity, and now you're admitting to taking away my pain. What darken touched you?" Then a thought hit me. "You aren't just fully blessed, are you? You are a Nephilim, too."

He nodded. "There are a few of us running around."

Of course he was a Nephilim. I didn't know why I hadn't connected the dots sooner.

A smile touched his face. "We need to hurry. I'll go first."

He cut the palm of his hand then handed me the blade. I hesitated before I slid the cold metal across my palm. The moment his hand grasped mine, my pain faded, and my heart felt like a ball of yarn was being wrapped around it, tightening ever so often to make sure that it wouldn't come unraveled. He said a few more words, and then I knew the binding was complete, because his lust hit me like a ton of bricks. Or was it my lust? I couldn't decipher my thoughts from his.

I shifted again on his lap, causing him to wince. My eyes widened after what I had just felt. There was no doubt that the commander was definitely hot for the pupil.

"I think I should … um … Maybe I should just …" I went to move off his lap, causing him to now groan.

He looked like he was about to lose control, and the thought that my nearness was the cause of that made me giddy.

I looked over his perfect physique. And he clenched his fist in his lap.

His voice was deeper than normal when he said, "Walls, Gabriella. Build them."

Embarrassed, I quickly tried to shut him out. "No offense, Commander, but your lust is hitting me pretty hard, so maybe you should build your own walls."

"Trying," he gritted out.

I couldn't help the smile that lit my face. Yeah, I was a little embarrassed that Finn knew how damn hot I thought he was, but it looked like we were in the same boat. Except he was having a hard time steering his ship.

Giving him some space, I stood up and walked to the massive bookshelf. I ran my hands over a golden book, trailing my fingers down the spine and accidentally hitting a small lever. Pressing it, the fake book opened, revealing the treasures hidden inside a box. There was an emerald ring that reminded me of Finn's eyes, a packet of notes that looked like love letters, and a lock of hair.

I lightly touched the deep brown lock of hair that was tied with a red ribbon.

"What are you doing?" a voice boomed from over my shoulder, causing me to almost drop the box.

"I'm sorry. I just saw the book and …" I closed the box quickly. "I'm sorry."

He took the box from me. "Careful, those things are priceless."

"Yeah, of course they are. I had no right. I'm sorry. I really am."

I watched him as he placed the box high on the top shelf, way out of my reach, making me feel even worse. Then he went into the kitchen, shoulders tense.

I followed him, pulling out a chair at the table. "I really am sorry. I didn't know that it held personal belongings."

He released a deep sigh. "I'm not mad. Those items just bring back a slew of emotions."

I thought of the ring. "Were they your mother's?"

"No."

My heart tightened. A lover, then?

"Oh." Was that the only word I could come up with?

My mind ran wild. You wouldn't keep belongings like that if your loved one was still breathing.

Curiosity getting the best of me, I couldn't help my next question. "What happened to her?"

He slammed a plate that had a peanut butter and jelly sandwich on it down in front of me. "She died."

His wall collapsed just for a brief second, and the grief

that I felt rode over me like a tidal wave, pulling me under to where, if he hadn't reinforced his walls quickly, I might not have ever surfaced.

I grabbed my plate and headed back toward the living room where I ate, even though I was no longer hungry. Finn's pain was so raw that his loss must've been very recent.

My emotions switched gears. To be the recipient of that kind of love was unfathomable. My stomach rolled. Surely, I wasn't jealous of a ghost?

The atmosphere had changed. I had invaded Finn's privacy and made him upset. After the binding, I was struggling with keeping my walls maintained.

I finished my sandwich in record time and put my plate in the sink. "I'm super tired. I guess the adrenaline from the confrontation with Devon has worn off. I think I'll head back to my dorm and maybe take a nap."

He knew I was lying, but he shooed me out of his house with the wolf on my heels.

Later that night, I watched a funny movie with Hannah and Trev, along with most of the students. No one had mentioned Devon's name. If they knew what had happened to him, I would have been shocked. It was like Finn had just made him disappear.

At some point during the show, I felt Finn show up. I knew exactly where he stood without even looking. However, feeling awkward after the day we had, I ignored him.

I got multiple strange looks about the wolf that refused to leave my side. I had whispered to Hannah that I would tell her later, but poor Trev was flabbergasted, especially when he tried to get super close to me on the blanket that I had lain out and the wolf came in between us. I looked up to find Finn's eyes on me and, not for the first time, thought he was communicating with the wolf.

When the movie was over and I was in my bed, I prepared myself for a dream, hoping that it would be yet another missing puzzle piece about my previous life. Regrettably, for whatever reason, no dreams came to me that night.

I should have had a restful sleep. Instead, I woke up feeling hollow.

twenty-six

THE HOLIDAYS WERE ALMOST NONEXISTENT. There was no time off from training or classes. It didn't bother me that there was no celebration, though. After all, I had been a foster kid. It was rare that I participated in Christmas festivities anyway.

As New Year's Day approached, I became more and more anxious. I had briefed both my besties on who my mother was and how I had been touched by more than just a few archangels. Seven to be exact. I also told them about how Azrael had put the Flaming Sword in me.

They were quiet, shocked, and mad that I had kept this a secret from them, but in the end, they had forgiven me and had numerous questions. Some, I still couldn't answer.

As my birthday approached, Hannah was terrified, and even Remy wasn't her usual ghostly self. None of us knew

if I'd be able to hide my powers.

Finn didn't voice his concerns, but he had me training in hand-to-hand and weapons three times a day. I was constantly tired and sore, but I had to admit that the training was paying off. I had gotten deadly accurate with the throwing knives.

Today, my morning classes had gone by faster than normal, maybe because I had been daydreaming about the archangels and not what Mrs. Fields was saying. Regardless, the day had escaped me.

In magic class, Finn had asked me numerous times if I was paying attention. I tried to keep my anxiety down and my walls built so he wouldn't be privy to my thoughts, but I felt like I was losing the battle.

Later that day, the wolf and I took the familiar path to his house and knocked on his cabin door several times. When there was no answer, I entered, calling out a couple of times for the commander. When he didn't respond, I still let myself in and shut the door behind me.

I looked at the clock on the wall. I was right on time for our hand-to-hand training. I knew he was in the cabin, because the binding was like a GPS system—I could always tell exactly where he was.

As I neared the couch, I heard the shower running. I plopped down, closing my eyes for a few seconds. All the extra training was exhausting.

The wolf stretched lazily in front of the fireplace, gently snoring.

I was almost asleep when I heard a noise.

I popped my eyes open to see Finn standing in front of me in nothing but a fluffy towel hanging low on his hips, water droplets dripping down his well-defined torso. Roaming my greedy eyes all over him, I hadn't had the chance to make it to his face yet when he cleared his voice. I jerked my eyes to his.

"Uh …" So articulate, but Lord help me, I had lost my knowledge of any and all vocabulary. He was magnificent.

A scowl masked his handsome face. "Sorry, I was out on the field, training some demis with props, when one of them exploded. I needed a shower and must've lost track of time."

"Hmm …" Still, no words.

"Let me go get changed."

"Yep." Yes! There was a complete word, and it was an appropriate one to use.

As soon as his nice, firm butt cleared the room, I took a couple of deep breaths. Seeing the most handsome man in the world in a towel? Of course I could handle that, duh. And when he came back into the room, I would use big girl sentences, and my eyes would stay on his face.

I fanned myself while making sure those damn walls were intact. Not that it mattered. I was pretty sure he had seen the drool coming out of my mouth a minute ago.

My eyes were closed again when Finn re-entered the room.

"You're exhausted," he said.

Without opening my eyes, I replied, "Yeah."

I heard him sit on the coffee table in front of the couch. "I'd like to give you the day off, but with your birthday approaching, I fear we don't have the time to slack."

I grunted.

"We could do something a little different today, though."

I opened my eyes. "Yes, you have my attention."

"And I'm not in a towel, imagine that."

Heat rose to my cheeks. "That's not my fault. You put a cute boy in a towel in front of me, and I'm probably going to look."

"Just cute? You were leering."

I narrowed my eyes into slits.

He chuckled, putting his hands up in a defensive pose. "Easy. If it were reversed, I would have been leering, too."

"I wasn't leering. I was just shocked. And you've seen me in a robe."

"I know. I leered."

I didn't know where this conversation was going, or how I should feel about it. Excited? Or should I exit stage right? I mean, he was still in mourning, or so it appeared.

He reached out to touch my leg, his warm palm sending tingles up my thigh. "Some of the fully blessed and demis, who are strong, have a get-together around this time in the training room. They fight one another."

"For fun?"

He laughed. "It's actually good training. Do you want to go?"

"I guess. I mean, if you think it'll help."

"It can't hurt." He stood then pulled me to my feet. "We need to leave now if we're going."

I tiredly followed him across campus to the training room. He held the door open for me, where I almost backpedaled when I saw Marlie-Beth over in the corner, laughing like a hyena. Her little side-kick, Angelina, was being the perfect puppet, laughing along with her at all the right times.

Finn trailed his hand up and down my spine. "Don't be nervous. Use Chamuel's gift of intuition and study your partner. You'll know what they plan before they do."

I gave a nod.

Finn pushed me farther into the room then went over to a sign-up board and put my name on the list.

One of the kids whined, "Commander, you can't fight. That's not fair."

Finn leveled him with a look. "I didn't add my name, but now that you've suggested it, maybe I should."

The whole class groaned, causing Finn to laugh.

We stood around the ring and watched as Dan called two fighters up at a time. The goal was to knock the other person out of the ring.

I wiped my sweaty palms on my pants. I could do this. I had been training so hard.

Dan gave me a wink when he called my name.

I took off my shoes and socks before I stepped into the center of the ring. Then my spine straightened when he called out Marlie-Beth's name.

"I'm a fully blessed," she spat. "Why would I lower myself to fight with a demi?"

Finn spoke up. "If you're too scared, Dan can call another name."

There were a few snickers.

Her face was red with rage as she stepped into the ring.

I calmed my heart and cleared my brain as Dan counted down. I stood still, waiting for her to come near me. I was not going to dance around and chase her.

Studying her stance like Finn had trained me to do, I watched as she threw a couple of warm-up punches to gage the distance between us. She always stepped with the front foot before she swung. Good to know.

Before Dan said *one*, Marlie-Beth swung. I barely had time to duck. Then she brought her knee up and caught me in the chin. I staggered back then dropped to a knee as she charged me. Dropping back on my hands, I kicked my leg out, aiming for her knee cap. The scream that tore from her lips gave me motivation.

I stood quickly and gave her a right jab before stepping on my right foot and pivoting on my left. Bringing my back to her front, I elbowed her in her face before I grabbed her in headlock and threw her over my shoulder and out of the circle. I was panting, but I had done it.

A slow clap started. I followed the sound to a smiling Finn.

All of a sudden, blackness started to cloud my sight. I

knew I was in danger before the visions started clawing at my brain. My knees hit the mat as I cradled my head, demons all over me, clawing at my flesh and trying to pull my limbs from my body. I screamed as one bit a chunk out of my neck, and the vein ruptured, blood spewing everywhere. They were killing me.

I barely recognized Dan as he rushed to my side, telling me, "It's an illusion."

He was right; this wasn't real. Just as I convinced myself to push the images out, my vision cleared enough for me to see Finn haul Marlie-Beth up to her feet. The demons had stopped mauling me but didn't release me.

Finn gave Marlie-Beth a shake that had her head flopping back and forth. "Release her."

Blood trickled down her face as she glared at me. Soon, the visions stopped completely, and I fell back on my bottom. Sweat was dripping down my spine.

Finn's voice was chilling when he told her, "You know the rules; no powers allowed in these fights. You lost, and like a coward, you attacked her. Get it together, or I'll remove you from the academy."

Her eyes widened in fear. "But where will I go?"

He shrugged. "Not my problem, but I hear Empowered Academy is always taking in kids with less than redeeming qualities." He dropped her to the ground. "Dan, take her off the remaining fight schedules. If she can't play by the rules, then she is not welcome in the ring."

I made my way to my feet. A couple of students patted

me on the back and told me congratulations.

There was nothing more I wanted to do than leave with my tail between my legs, but I couldn't give Marlie-Beth the satisfaction. So, taking a deep breath, I looked at the small crowd and asked, "So, who's next?"

Finn laughed as Dan called out the next two on the list. I made myself watch the next few fights before I excused myself, weaving my way through the students.

A large hand hit the door, opening it for me. I looked up to see Finn smiling down at me.

"You did good."

I blew a piece of stray hair out of my face. "I have a good teacher."

My wolf, who had been waiting patiently for me outside the door, nuzzled my leg. I pet him absentmindedly.

I didn't know if Finn could read the expression on my face, or if he could feel from the binding that I needed some quiet time to myself. Either way, he said, "See you tomorrow."

I waved as I walked past him. At least I no longer had the hunky teacher's image of him standing in a towel in the forefront of my mind. I had a feeling that trick of Marlie-Beth's was going to give me nightmares tonight. Illusion or not, I still felt the demons' hands on me.

My life was already hectic enough without adding nightmares of damn demons to it.

twenty-seven

WHEN I GOT BACK TO my dorm, Hannah and Remy were there. After I told them about the stunt that Marlie-Beth had pulled, they decided what we needed the most was a sleepover. We gossiped and laughed and pretended that we weren't all scared about my approaching birthday. At some point, we fell asleep.

The next morning, I got up like it was my execution day instead of my birthday.

Upon awakening, we found a package with a note that said I had been cordially invited as a demi to come to the New Year's Day party. This was the one day of the year where all demis and fully blessed could come together, no matter their ranking or what year they were at the academy.

I laid a hand on my belly and looked at Remy. "Man, I

am so nervous. I'm scared my powers are going to come to me while I'm in the middle of the dance floor. You're going with me, right?"

"Duh. And we've been over this a thousand times. When your powers hit you, we will get you out of there."

Hannah nodded. "Our goal has never been to hide your powers completely. We just don't want everyone to know how valuable you really are."

"Yeah, you know. We don't want to wave a homemade banner that screams, '*I'm a Nephilim coming into my powers. Also, I'm literally the Flaming Sword.*' Then in smaller print '*But I'm pretending to be a demi.*'"

Remy clapped her hands. "Enough chitchat. Hurry up and get changed. Your hair is begging me to style it in a Dutch braid."

I shuffled toward the bathroom.

"Oh, and Gabriella, the hot commander left you a package at the door this morning. Being the wonderful snoop that I am, I opened it and hung it up for you. It's in the bathroom."

I looked at the tight black dress that was hung up on the back of the door. It was simple, sleek, and beautiful. There were matching stilettos, too. I sighed happily. Finn was hot, powerful, and thoughtful. I had to watch it around him, or my lust was going to turn into love if I wasn't careful.

After taking a quick shower, I slid the dress on. Running my hands over the fabric, I came to the realization that tonight was either going to be a night for the history books or a cringe-worthy experience. I had a feeling there would be no in-between.

The moment we entered the auditorium, I felt Finn. He was somewhere toward the back, and his presence immediately made me more comfortable.

Hannah tugged me along as music blared and bodies smashed together in rhythm. As soon as we were on the dance floor, Remy made her excuses and headed for the DJ booth.

After a few fast songs, Hannah pushed me toward the bar. "There is no drinking age at the academy. Let's order something."

I wasn't sure if that was wise, not with my powers coming to me fully at some point. So, though I took the drink she handed me, I barely sipped from it.

A hand fell on my back. Turning, I saw Trev beaming down at me.

"Hey, beautiful. I couldn't take my eyes from you when you walked through the door."

A friend of his came up and slung an arm around Trev. "Yeah, he threatened the whole group to not stare at you, or he would personally take their eyes from their sockets."

I raised an eyebrow, and Trev blushed.

"That's a tad violent," I said.

He shrugged. "Want to dance?"

I looked at Hannah, who hopped onto a barstool. "Go have some fun. I'll be right here."

"Are you sure?" I asked.

"Of course I am."

I gave her a hug before I followed Trev to the dance floor. He pulled me into his arms with a little twirl.

"The last time I asked you to dance, I didn't get to hold you for very long, and then you disappeared."

I winced as I remembered that night. "Hopefully, I won't be running away from the academy tonight."

Trev was talking about his family back home when a wave of jealousy and anger hit me. My feet faltered for a bit before I continued to sway again in Trev's arms. I glanced over Trev's shoulder to see Finn up against a wall. A few girls were talking to him, trying to get his attention, but his eyes were glued to me.

Trev chucked me under the chin. His handsome face smiling. "Are you listening, or am I just rambling too much?"

"Sorry. I was just wondering if I should go check on Hannah," I lied.

He shook his head. "She'll be fine."

This time, I listened when he talked about his little sisters. It was clear that he adored them to no end. He was saying, "I would do anything in the world for the twins. Ever since my father died, I feel like it's up to me to protect them."

I patted his chest. Trev was such a sweet guy. "They are lucky to have you."

The music changed and, at the same moment, a wave

of heat washed over me, and the mother of all headaches started to rage.

I stopped dancing and rubbed my temples. "Holy hell. I've got a horrible headache. It must be all this loud music. I think I'm going to go find Hannah. Go mingle with everyone, and grace all the ladies with those adorable winks."

He laughed. "The only one I really care about is the one I'm holding on to."

Nausea hit me like a ton of bricks. "Oh, man, my head is pounding. Forgive me if I don't have a witty reply."

He gave me a concerned look. "Let me walk you back to your room."

"No, you're fine. Stay. I promised Hannah I'd get her before I left."

He acted like he didn't want to let me go, but I turned on my heel as fast as I could and headed through the crowd to the bar. People were jostling me left and right as pain radiated down my scalp. Just when I thought I was going to collapse, strong hands grabbed my waist.

"I can feel your pain. Can you walk out of here?" Finn's warm timber caressed my ear.

"Yeah, but we need to hurry."

We quickly made our way toward the door where my wolf met me. He nuzzled my hand for a second, knowing I was hurting.

Finn continued to half-drag me until we were outside. Then he slung me up into his arms.

My voice was slurred as I asked, "Is Champ following?"

"You named my wolf?"

"He's my wolf."

He chuckled. "Yeah, I guess he is. Don't worry; he's following." Finn's walls were down, and his worry was overwhelming me.

Along the way, I passed out a couple of times, and when Finn placed me on the bed, I immediately crawled into a fetal position.

He pointed at Champ. "Boy, lay down in front of the door and don't let anyone in unless it's Hannah or Remy."

"You think he can see Remy?" I panted out.

"I don't know about seeing her, but he can probably feel the air pressure change."

Champ did a couple of circles then blocked the door.

I was about to be deadly sick when Remy came barreling through the door. Then there was a knock. Finn let Hannah in.

"She's coming into her powers?" Hannah asked.

Finn nodded. "It's going to be bad. She was touched by so many archangels." The worry in his voice had Hannah tearing up.

Remy curled up behind me on the bed, laying an arm over me. Of course, it went right through me, leaving chills on my skin.

Finn was saying, "You two stay with her. I need to go back to the party for at least another thirty minutes. There were a few students who saw us leaving together, and she was really struggling with just walking. I'll go spread it around that she drank too much. Just in case."

Sweat started beading my brow, but I didn't say a word.

Finn left, and the last thing I remember was thinking my insides were on fire, and I was almost positive I was dying.

twenty-eight

VOICES WERE MAKING ME STIR. I swatted at the closest one.

My head pounded. I felt like I was about to throw up at any second, and no one would let a girl die in peace.

"How long has she been like this?"

"Since your perky little ass walked out that door. So ... twenty-five minutes," Remy said.

"Why didn't you come get me?"

"Look at me!" Remy shrieked. Of all the times she had to be a dramatic diva, why now? "I couldn't go to you like this. Thank goodness I have Ariel's talents. I was finally able to convince that fleabag to go and fetch you."

"And she did this to you?"

"Duh, pretty boy. Who else could have done this? I was holding her, and the next thing I knew ... *boom*."

I tried to sit up, but a large hand pushed me back down. "Rest, Maka."

That was easy to say, but I needed to see my friend. Something was obviously terribly wrong.

I opened my eyes to see Remy in full-on flesh. Then a wave of pain hit me, and she began to flicker.

"Oh shit, here we go again. She's got me flickering like a 1950's channel on the boob tube." She let out a deep sigh as I groaned.

I blacked out again during the worst of the pain, and I'd never been so thankful in my life.

The next time I woke, Finn was sitting at the end of my bed, his knees drawn up with more flexibility than a person his size should have been able to achieve. Hannah and Remy were curled up like cats on Remy's small twin bed.

I pulled myself up to a sitting position. "What happened?" I whispered.

"You got your powers."

"I know that, but"—I jerked my head toward Remy, who was currently in human form—"what did I do to Remy?"

"Apparently, you made her corporal. Not sure how long it'll last. Unfortunately, because she died before her eighteenth birthday, her powers hadn't come to her yet. Still, if we can figure out a way for her to become corporal at will, that could be her gift."

I gave a tired nod. "Yeah, that'd be cool."

"How are you feeling?"

"Like I've been run over."

I looked at Finn's tired face. He appeared exhausted. "How long have you been in here?"

He looked at this watch. Then he rested his head back on my wall. "Ten hours."

That would explain why my bladder felt like it was about to burst. "What do we do now?"

"We hide you until you are feeling better, and then we resume your training."

I looked over to where Remy and Hannah were still sleeping. Then I tried to sit up too fast and ended up falling into Finn. He wrapped his arms around me as I dropped my head to his chest.

As I snuggled deeper into his arms, I asked, "Do you ever feel like we've known each other before?"

He kissed the top of my head. "It does feel like that, doesn't it?"

Before I could doze off again, my bladder shot me a warning. "I need to use the restroom."

Within seconds, he was off the bed and had me in his arms. He placed me in the bathroom and shut the door.

As soon as I was done, I washed my hands then splashed cold water on my face. My legs started to wobble.

The door swung open. "You need me?"

Without waiting for me to answer, he picked me up and put me back in bed. As soon as he had me situated, he crawled over me and resumed his original spot. I tried not to sigh, but I was hoping he would hold me again.

I couldn't get comfortable. My back felt like I had been bit by several mosquitoes. It was itching and warm. I kept rubbing it along the sheets, but the pain wasn't going away.

"Finn? My back is itching. Horribly."

He gave me a sleepy smile. "That's what happens when you get your wings."

"You really think I'll get my wings?"

He nodded. "You're Nephilim. We will try to coax them out when we are by ourselves. The itching will go away in a few minutes."

His eyes were closing, and I found myself whispering, "You don't have to stay."

"That's what got me in trouble the first time. I've been paying for it ever since."

"What are you talking about?" I asked.

Finn looked so weary as he closed his beautiful eyes. "Do you know what I think, Maka? I think you need to sleep and pray for dreams."

"Maka? You've called me that before. What does it mean?"

A half-smile lit his handsome face. "If you truly want to know, then you will remember."

He stretched his big body closer to me, and my heart started pounding. He couldn't kiss me. I looked like death, and I hadn't brushed my teeth in almost eighteen hours.

Instead, with his big hand, he gently covered my face and closed my eyes. "Sleep, Maka."

I smiled as I scrunched under the covers.

Sometime later in the night, I felt Finn's body stretch out beside mine. His warmth cocooned me, and my restless sleep quickly turned into one of deep slumber. I had hoped to dream of Finn and how, if I imagined it just right, his gaze was one of longing and promises that a man like him would aim to keep. Those dreams weren't in the cards, though. Instead, I dreamt of present times and a fallen angel who was hell-bent on ruining anything that was blessed.

twenty-nine

MY DREAMS WERE ALL OVER the place. One right after another.

In one, I saw into the future where Camaella stood somewhere in the dirty streets of Los Angeles, commanding demons to do her bidding. The whole state of California was barely accessible. If you were human and wanted to enter the state, well, then you entered at your own peril and with the knowledge that you probably wouldn't be leaving the land of milk and honey. She stood there in an emerald green blouse and white pants, of all things. There was so much dirt all around her, yet not a spec on her pants. She shouted commands to demons that looked like humans, except for their black eyes. The rims were a faint red. She was planning on marching east. She had searched most of the West Coast and middle America for the academy and had come up empty-handed.

She stomped her Jimmy Choos on the broken pavement.

A demon crossed in front of her, and with a flick of her wrist, she had him flying through the air. He hit an upside-down car and was pinned between it and the power she was currently controlling him with.

"Gather everyone and tell them that we will be leaving in two hours. They have had enough fun. We must find the academy."

He grunted.

Taking that as affirmation, she released him from her hold, and he scurried around her, doing her bidding.

None of them understood. If they didn't find the academy before more of those little brats became immortal, all their hard work would be ruined. It had already been reported by an oracle that they had a chosen one in their midst. One who had been blessed by more than one angel. If you added an immortal of that kind of strength to the mix, the archangels could take their army of demis and destroy everything she had built so far. There was destruction, pain, and suffering everywhere she went.

If she didn't find that academy soon, Lucifer would kill her instead of making her queen. There was no way she was going to let some fully blessed teenagers take that away from her.

If the archangels had never interfered, she wouldn't be standing here today, in the middle of a warzone, with human flesh on the bottom of her designer shoes. It always seemed to go back to them. This was all their fault. She would personally find every single one of the fully blessed and kill them herself.

thirty

THE NEXT MORNING, WHEN I awoke, Finn and Hannah were gone. Remy was sitting in a chair, painting every other fingernail black.

"Oh, hey," she said. "So the girl that can make the dead visible is awake."

"Are you mad at me?" I asked.

"Hell no. Actually, your hot boyfriend and I talked this morning. I think, if I can get a handle on how to be solid when I want to be seen and invisible when I'm in stealth mode, then I can be a great advantage to my friends."

"He's not my boyfriend."

"Um, okkkuur. But all I'm saying, sista, is any man who keeps a watch over you while you sleep until he knows that you're going to be fine is probably just a little more than your teacher. That's all I'm saying. Okay, maybe not all.

I need to mention that I've caught you numerous times staring at him. I mean, it's no biggie, because who doesn't stare? Well, I guess I shouldn't while in solid form, but that's not the point. You love birds have it bad for each other."

Sitting here, arguing with my ghostly bestie, was going to get me nowhere. I decided to ignore her as I padded into the bathroom. I needed a shower. I felt so gross.

Taking a long, hot shower, I got myself together. Forty glorious minutes later, I was dressed in regular clothes—some skinny jeans and a plain white T-shirt.

I was going to skip my morning class. Instead of wasting away in Mrs. Fields' class, I needed to tell Finn of my dream. Camaella was desperate to find the academy, and once she did, it might be game over for all of us.

"Are you not going to class?" Remy asked.

"Nope."

"You've already missed a day."

I gave her my most *are you freaking serious?* look. "I just had a dream about Camaella." I quickly explained to her why that in itself was terrifying. "Usually, I have dreams of things that have already happened, but I guess coming into my powers has opened up some new doors. I had a dream of something that hasn't happened yet. Camaella will destroy California, and then, apparently, she is heading this way. So, in the scheme of things, I think it's okay if I skip that old hag's class."

"Um, yay, to the futuristic dreams. Sure that will come

in handy. And are you getting snarky with me?"

"I think so, yes."

"Okay, just checking." She waved me to the door. "I'm going to hide out here until we can figure out this whole how-to-make-me-invisible thing again."

"I'm sorry, Remy." I couldn't believe the things I was bitching about when she had bigger issues. "I was inconsiderate."

"Of course you were. That's why we're friends. Also, if I can figure all this out, it'll be like I, too, have another chance at life." A beautiful smile came across her face. "Now, I'm about to shave my legs for the first time in forever, so go find your lover, and don't forget to take your wolf with you."

I gave Remy a quick hug and tried to hide my shock as her body didn't pass through mine. "Come on, Champ, let's go."

Power strummed through me like a current. I had so much energy that it was hard not to bounce on my toes. I felt more alive than I'd ever felt.

"Champ, let's go see Finn," I told him once we got outside.

The wolf put his gray snout in the air and sniffed several times before he started to trot through the courtyard. The minute he turned onto the familiar, narrow trail, I rubbed his head.

Right before we got to the cabin, Champ started growling with his tail tucked between his legs. The front door to Finn's was cracked.

Something was wrong. I could feel it.

A few seconds later, I heard someone coming from around the back of the cabin. I tensed before I felt the pull in my belly. Seconds later, Finn appeared.

He held up a finger, signaling for me to be quiet. Then he crept toward the cracked open door and slipped inside without making a noise.

I should have waited outside, but after several minutes, I decided to go in after him.

I gasped when I stepped over the threshold. His place was trashed. The coffee table and ottoman were turned over, the couches were ripped apart, and broken dishes lay everywhere. There were no books on the shelf. Instead, they lay scattered everywhere, all except one. The golden one that held his keepsakes.

"They took the book." He slammed his fist against an overturned table. "Did you tell anyone?"

"Not a soul."

"Are you sure about that?"

"Positive."

"What are you doing here?"

I stopped from picking up a shredded pillow. "What? Now I'm a suspect?"

He ran a hand down his face. "No, of course not. This is just not good. Whoever stole the keepsake book knew that it was important to me." I watched as he kicked an upside-down table out of his way.

"I get that your loved one's belongings were important to you, but why would they be important to anyone else?" I asked.

"It wouldn't be important to anyone else. They took it because they are trying to figure me out."

"I don't understand,"

"You wouldn't." He threw a chair across the room, causing me to flinch. "I want that book back, but I can't let anyone know how important it is to me."

"We'll get it back," I promised.

He gave me a nod.

I bent down and started picking up the books laying on the floor, returning them to the shelf.

"You don't have to help me clean."

"You watched over me while I was at my worst. I think helping you clean your house is the least I could do."

When he gave me a smile, I was shocked at where my line of thinking went. I wanted him to kiss me.

I was in the middle of craziness, and my hormones were running rampant.

"When do you think the book with the items was stolen?" I asked.

"I don't know."

"Because you were with me?"

He didn't answer, and he didn't have to.

We cleaned for an hour in complete silence. After I hauled another trash bag to the door, I told him about my dream. The only sign that he heard me was his body becoming rigid, and I could feel his anger through the binding that connected us.

It was late by the time we got his cabin back to normal. Then he walked me and Champ back to my dorm.

Outside the door, he asked, "Have you had the urge to let your wings out yet?"

I shook my head.

"Let's see if we can fix that tomorrow. If you can learn how to control them, they won't make random appearances."

I laughed. "That would totally blow my demi cover, wouldn't it? I'm kind of excited to see them."

He tucked a piece of hair behind my ear. "You should be."

"What color do you think they will be?"

"The colors are different shades of grey or black."

"What color are yours?"

He looked around the empty hall before he gave me a quick kiss on the forehead. "I'll show you tomorrow as soon as the sun comes up. Sleep tight, Maka."

My heart sighed with happiness as I closed the door. Tomorrow was going to be awesome. I wasn't even upset that it'd be the weekend and I'd be working.

I took a quick shower then crawled into the bed with a snoring Champ right beside me, silently vowing to help Finn find that keepsake book.

To be loved so fiercely, even after death, by Finn, was an honor.

Not for the first time did I find myself jealous of his lover's ghost.

thirty-one

THE NEXT DAY, I WAS up before my alarm went off. Not really knowing what to expect, I put on a pair of yoga pants and a T-shirt. Then I kissed a sleeping Remy on her head and snuck out of the dorm. Champ was on my heels as I jogged toward Finn's cabin.

Finn was waiting for me when I arrived at his place. Walls up, I drank in the sight of him. His T-shirt was snug over his body, and a pair of sweatpants left little to the imagination.

He was zipping a backpack, not looking at me when he asked, "You ready?"

I bounced on the balls of my feet. "So ready."

He laughed. "Champ has to stay here, okay?"

I scratched behind the wolf's ears. "Did you hear that, boy? I have to leave you, but I'll be back soon."

Champ gave me a lick on hand then went to lie down in front of the fire. Obviously, he was okay with being left behind.

Finn grabbed my hand and took me outside. "We're going to the west of the property, at the very edge. There is a mountain that we will be on the top of."

"So, we're hiking there?"

His green eyes twinkled as he handed me the backpack, and then I watched in fascination as he took his T-shirt off before stuffing it in the side of the backpack that I was still holding. My mouth dropped open.

He took a step closer, and I could feel his body radiating heat. I looked up his chiseled torso, passed his masculine jaw, and to those hypnotizing green eyes of his that were full of lust.

He stopped when there was a mere three inches that separated us. Then, in the blink of an eye, his wings popped out. They were as magnificent as the man who stood in front of me. Feathery and at least six feet wide, they looked as strong as they were beautiful. His black wings matched the same color as the tattoos that swirled around his arms and lightly up his neck.

I started to reach out to touch them when he snagged my hand with a shake of his head.

"Maka, to touch another angel's wings is like foreplay for humans."

I felt my face redden.

He kissed the back of my hand before he laid it on his

chest. Then he grasped my chin and forced my head up. "You can touch them any time you want. I just thought I should forewarn you of the significance first." Then he wrapped both arms around my waist and pulled me flush against his body. "You ready?"

"For what?"

With a wicked smile, he scooped me up into his arms and ran until his wings carried us into the sky. I let out a shout as I tightly looped my arms around his neck and buried my head against him.

He laughed as we soared. "Come now, Maka. Since when have you been afraid of a little adventure?"

I slowly peeked out. We were flying over the treetops. The wind against my face felt so freeing. As he circled around, I laughed.

"Don't you drop me," I warned as he dove down toward a lake just to swoop back up at the last second.

"Never."

He slowed as we neared the mountain top. My face felt wind burned, but I didn't care. I was laughing as he gently put me on my feet.

His expression was so tender that I felt the binding around my heart tighten. I wanted to see my wings, to learn to fly. But more than anything, I wanted to feel his lips on mine.

His gaze turned hungry before he did crash his lips against mine.

This wasn't just a kiss. This was a deep yearning that was

finally being fulfilled. How had I lasted this long without knowing his taste?

He pressed into me further as he deepened the kiss, and all rational thoughts left my mind. As his tongue met mine, my heart ached with a burning need. He clutched my hips as a growl vibrated in his chest. That sound was the sexiest thing I had ever heard. Then, with one last kiss, he pulled back from me.

My breath was coming in pants. I felt my swollen lips as he closed his eyes and gritted his teeth, clearly trying to get ahold of himself.

Finally, he said, "That wasn't the lesson I planned on giving you."

I shrugged. "I might have liked it better than the flying."

His laugh turned into a sigh. "Okay, Maka, turn around."

I did as he asked.

He swept my hair over my shoulder. "Do you feel this?" He was rubbing between my shoulder blades.

"Yeah, it feels warmer there than anywhere else on my body."

He continued to rub my back. "Close your eyes and concentrate on letting that warmth spread out."

I did as he asked. With my mind, I pushed the centralized warmth out toward my fingertips. Then I heard a *woosh* and a *snap*, followed by Finn's gasp. There was no pain. Unfurling my wings felt just like raising my arm or kicking out my leg.

Without opening my eyes, I asked, "Is there something wrong?"

"No, Maka. You are the most beautiful creature I have ever seen."

He gave me the courage I needed to open my eyes and look over my shoulder.

I was shocked. My wings weren't massive like Finn's—half the size, actually—but they were just as magnificent, and they were crimson red.

"I have a feeling that's not normal."

"Not at all," he said. "But just like everything else about you, your wings are extraordinary. Let's work on retracting them."

After a few tries, I learned how to put my wings away.

"You ready to fly?"

I looked over the cliff that we stood on. "Um ... no, not really."

He grasped my hand. "I will never let you fall. Trust me?"

I wouldn't have nodded if I had known what he would do next.

Finn tossed me over the cliff, and I screamed as I kicked and flayed mid-air. I was falling. Panic seized my heart.

A shadow came barreling beside me at the speed of a bullet.

Finn yelled, "Use your wings."

I let the warmth spread out and heard the pop as a flash of red came into my peripheral vision. Naturally, they began to beat, keeping me suspended in air. My laughter quickly turned into anger as I saw the smirking Finn beside me.

"You jerk!"

"Retaliation?" He tilted his head with the question. "I will let you toss me from the cliff if you can catch me."

The next thirty minutes was spent with me chasing after Finn as he dived and soared around every obstacle we flew over and around. With this little game, he was getting me used to my wings.

"Time out," I shouted. I was never going to catch that man.

He circled around and flew toward me. Grabbing me in the air, he pulled me up against him. The sun was fading as we hovered there, watching it disappear behind the mountains. I wanted to remember this moment forever. Him holding me tightly, our wings surrounding, us suspended in the air ... It was perfection.

He gently kissed me. It didn't have the heat of our first kiss, but it was no less priceless.

When he dropped me off at my dorm, having insisted on flying me back, since it was important that no one know that I had wings, much less red wings, the ball of yarn that was binding us together pulsed with an emotion. I built my walls and did my best to hide the shock I was feeling Because ... with that one emotion that had slipped through, he had let me know that he loved me.

Today had been the best day of my life.

thirty-two

I WENT TO BED THAT night, dreaming of a fully blessed who had somehow managed to sneak his way into my heart. My dreams took me to a past life, one that I had been craving to see ever since I had learned that I had lived in another time.

I stood in a meadow of black-eyed Susan's. My white dress blew around my ankles as the gentle breeze picked up. With my palms, I covered my eyes as I counted backward from twenty. When I heard a noise to my left, I couldn't help but giggle.

"Ready or not, here I come," I called.

I moved through the meadow, looking for the one who held my heart. Where did he go? His muscular body was hard to hide, so his only option would have been to find an astronomically large object to hide behind.

Over to the left of the meadow was a bank that led to the small creek. As I started to head that way, I heard a noise behind me, alerting me that I was going the wrong way. I whirled just in time to be tackled to the grass, warm arms cushioning my fall. Before I could even reprimand my love, his lips were on mine.

Every kiss was like the first. He demanded my soul, and my soul was his for the taking.

He glided his hand down my side, causing me to shudder. His touch could do that to me—make me burn with a fever that always left me yearning for more.

He tore his lips from mine too soon, and I groaned.

He laughed as he whispered, "I love you more and more every day, Ella."

The dream started to fade as I recalled that Sandalphon had once called me that. Ella.

I tried to get the dream to return to me. I wanted—no, needed—to see the boy's face who was my other half, but something was pulling me out of my dream.

I woke up to Champ pawing at my chest and Remy screaming for my help.

I bolted upright in bed. "What's going on?"

"There is a fight going on. I think Hannah is in trouble."

I threw on a pair of sweatpants and didn't bother with shoes as I ran out of my dorm room. The halls were crowded, and students wouldn't get out of my way, even with the wolf nipping at their heels. I elbowed my way through all the first-year students and took the stairs leading up to the second floor where Hannah's room was.

I momentarily froze in the doorway when I saw blood everywhere.

A warm hand grabbed me by the elbow. "Gabriella, go back downstairs," Trev said.

I shook my head as I continued to look for my friend. There were at least twenty kids fighting each other in the small dorm hallway.

Remy floated by me. "Hurry up. She needs us."

I shoved away from Trev, and when he tried to grab me, I twisted so I could avoid his grasp. Running after Remy, I was horrified at what I saw.

Angelina and a boy named Zack had Hannah pinned against the wall with a blade against her throat.

Someone was screaming. It took me a moment to realize it was me.

"We need to help her!" Remy snapped me out of it.

A loud commotion made me look behind me to see Trev fighting with another student. The student had a medium-sized blade, and Trev was barehanded. Still, he seemed to be deflecting the blows pretty easily.

I moved forward through the crowd until I finally stood before Angelina and Zack.

"Guys what are you doing? Let Hannah go."

Angelina turned toward me. Her eyes held all the malice in the world in them.

I gasped. "You both are darken."

Her manic laughed caused chill bumps to rise on my

arms. "Oh, let's not put labels on us."

Zack snorted. "We are fully blessed who have chosen the right path."

I held my hands up. "It doesn't matter what you are. Release Hannah."

A smile lit Angelina's face. "She wants us to release her friend."

Zack pushed the blade in his hand deeper against Hannah's neck. "I think we can do that."

Hannah's blue eyes met mine with a plea as I stood there and watched them slit her throat.

A rage like no other bubbled up inside of me. Everything went completely dark inside of me like I was shutting down.

Not caring who saw I had power, I attacked. My movements were quick as I dislodged the knife from Zack, punched him in the nose, and then rammed the heel of my hand at his broken nose. The bone splintered toward his brain.

I watched as he sunk to his knees, but somehow, he was still alive. Because he was immortal.

All my anger and rage manifested into a tight ball. I shoved my wrath toward him, and a brilliant white light hit him square in the chest. His eyes turned vacant before he hit the floor.

Angelina jumped onto my back. Grabbing a fistful of her hair, I threw her over my shoulder, and as soon as she hit the ground, I stepped around her, heading toward my friend.

I watched as Trev came up and knelt next to Angelina. He withdrew a blade and stabbed her in the heart. Then his eyes met mine briefly. "You'll thank me later."

I didn't know what he meant, and I didn't care. One of my best friends was lying in a fetal position, holding her neck. Her eyes were glassy, and she was in pain.

Trev said, "You obviously have the power to heal her, so do it."

I didn't hesitate. I removed her hands and pushed mine against her wound. The blood made it slippery, but I didn't let go as I sat there and concentrated on healing my friend.

I felt something inside of me shift. My power was bubbling up to the surface. Raphael had blessed me with the power, and I was about to make use of it.

My palm started to warm, and Hannah twitched underneath of me. She tried to move, so I placed my knee on her chest. She cried out in pain, but I refused to release her. Only when the heat in my palm died down did I remove my hand. Her wound wasn't deep anymore. It probably didn't even need stitches.

Her blue eyes fluttered before she passed out.

Remy came floating over and was cooing words to Hannah, even though she wasn't awake. I wasn't sure if I could lift Hannah even with my powers. As tall as she was, she had thirty pounds on me. So, I grabbed her by her arms and started to drag her through the chaos. I was so focused on getting Hannah somewhere safe that I didn't hear Marlie-Beth come up behind me.

Her hand was making an arch down toward my chest, and I barely registered she held a knife, when an arrow whistled through the air, striking her in the middle of the forehead. It seemed as if the world stopped for a few moments as I watched the light fade out of her eyes before she hit the ground.

I swiveled my head to where the arrow had been released. Finn stood there with his feet braced apart, looking rumpled from sleep. He had just saved my life.

Hannah moaned as I continued to drag her through the kids that were still fighting one another. Poor Remy was having a panic attack, flickering in and out of visibility.

A boy in my weapons training class pointed at me as I was weaving in and out of students who were throwing punches at one another. "You are what the boss is looking for." He reared back to throw the blade in his hands.

I heard Finn and Trev shout, but it was too late. I felt the sting of metal as the blade hit under my collarbone and above my right breast. The boy might not have been the best in the class, but he always made his mark. That's how I knew he didn't want to kill me. He just wanted to wound me.

Without meaning to, I collapsed like a broken doll onto Hannah.

Then I saw the boy hit the ground, his dead eyes staring into mine.

The darken probably shouldn't have sent mortals in to be their spies. They just lost a soldier.

My body was lifted as darkness swarmed around me. I had my powers now, so why wasn't I healing quickly?

I heard someone say, "Sir, I think that's the last of the darken. The immortals aren't dead, just immobilized."

Finn lightly squeezed me in his arms. "Good. Take them to the basement. I'll deal with them in a second. Also, have someone grab Hannah and carry her to the infirmary."

Then I heard Trev say, "You know this is just the beginning. They will not stop."

"Shut the hell up!" Finn shouted as he carried me through the hall. "I won't lose her again."

Trev said, "What if you already have?"

Finn stopped walking. For a second there, I thought he was going to put me down to pummel Trev into the ground, but when I let out a whimper, he got his feet moving again.

"Rest, Maka."

I closed my eyelids, knowing that I was safe in his arms.

I awoke to the sound of a machine beeping. Finn was sitting in a chair beside where I lay. Blood was spattered all over him. Whether it was mine, someone else's, or both, I didn't know.

A smile lit his face when he saw me staring at him. "Hey, you."

"Hannah?" My voice was hoarse.

"Thanks to you, her wounds are almost non-existent. She is asleep in your dorm room with Remy. I figured, between Remy and the wolf watching her, she'd be pretty safe."

I nodded. His emotions were so heavy that they were slapping up against the wall I was trying to build mentally. Then, trying to make a joke, I said, "Well, it looks like I'm still alive."

"You're immortal now. The only thing that can kill you is inside of you." He sounded so gruff that I sat up in bed and started detaching the wires from me.

I looked over at him. "None of this is your fault."

He didn't acknowledge me.

"I'm fine. I've already healed. I don't need all this."

He nodded. "I know. But I'm still trying to keep up appearances."

I winced. "I think it's too late for that. I think … I know I killed Zack with my powers."

He ran a hand over his face. When he didn't say anything, I grew nervous.

Shifting the hospital gown to cover more of me, I asked, "Why were those kids attacked?"

"There were eleven kids in that hall, alone, who would be turning immortal soon. I don't think the darken were supposed to attack. Maybe they were trying to prove their worth to the Empowered Academy? I'm not sure," he said tiredly.

"Did you know that there were darken supporters in the academy?"

His green eyes met mine. "My darker side recognized them for what they were. I knew they were heavily blessed by the darken. They came before you were here, so I wanted to give them a chance to do the right thing, to choose the right side. I didn't know they had already chosen their side. They think I know where the Flaming Sword is and that I'll lead them right to it."

"Who? The darken?" I asked.

"More specifically, my father." He stretched his long legs out in front of him. "The angel I was born from. My father wasn't part of the fifteen, but he was still an angel. One of the many differences between us is he abandoned my mother and me after he sired me. He didn't show interest in me until he realized how powerful I am."

As I stared into his green eyes, it hit me. Those piercing green eyes. Smoldering good looks. I had seen them in my dreams. "You are Lucifer's son."

He clenched his jaw. "Not my proudest admission."

I got up from the bed, making sure to keep my gown closed behind me as I knelt at his feet. I placed one hand on his knee. "It doesn't matter who you come from. A wise person once told me that we all had a choice. We could choose who we want to be."

He smiled. Then he snagged my waist and pulled me onto his lap. He ran his hands softly over my face before his lips met mine. He kissed me as if he had kissed me a thousand times before. He knew exactly when to be tender and when to manipulate my lips into giving him more.

The tug that I had always felt when he was near raged inside of me as if it were a cheetah that had been caged too long. As he deepened the kiss, I felt the beast inside of me flick its tail along the bars of my heart. It wanted out of its small confinement, and it wanted to let the commander in.

When he pulled back from me, ending the kiss, I couldn't help but sway into him.

He chuckled. "I have to go take care of something. Come with me?"

I couldn't speak. Not yet. Instead, I just nodded as he grabbed my hand and pulled me to my feet. He then waited for me to change clothes before ushering me out of the medical building.

We set off through the courtyard, my senses so hyper-aware that it was almost sensory overload.

He gave my hand a squeeze. "You'll learn to control your powers."

Finally, we stopped when we saw Dan patrolling the borders.

"Did he escape?" Finn asked.

Dan nodded. "Sorry, sir."

Finn clenched his jaw as he turned on his heel, pulling me behind him as he led me toward my dorm.

"Who escaped?"

"Trev."

"I don't understand. Why would Trev escape?"

"Because he knows that you're not just a demi. He knows that we're hiding something." Anger rolled off

Finn. "I should have handled him right then, but I needed to see about your injuries. If he's escaped, then it's a matter of time before demons show up here."

We went up the steps to my dorm so fast that I wasn't entirely sure my feet touched the ground. We turned down the hall and all but bumped into Richard.

He looked down at our clasped hands and gave me a wink. "Sir, I've made sure that the dorms are secure. I believe we should take to the skies and get an aerial view."

Finn looked at me and hesitated.

I put my hands on his chest. "Remember, you said that some things need to be kept a secret. I can't go with you."

Whether Trev knew that I was different or not wasn't as big of a concern as him knowing that I was different enough to have red wings.

Finn nodded. "You're right. Do not leave your room."

"I won't."

"Hannah has been deposited in your room, along with Champ. Between them and Remy, you should be safe." He distractedly kissed the top of my head before he left with Richard by his side.

Remy gave me a wide-eyed look as she floated next to me. "What in the ever-loving hell is going on?"

I rubbed my arms. The chill was seeping into me, and I couldn't seem to stop shaking. "The short version is Lucifer is Finn's dad. He sent darken here to spy on the academy." I looked over to see a sleeping Hannah. She looked peaceful. I said a silent prayer, thanking the heavens that my friend was still alive.

Remy became corporal in front of my eyes before she threw herself at me. "Oh, girl, I was so scared. Hannah was bleeding, you were bleeding, and there were dead kids laying in the halls. I know I'm dead, but that really messed with me."

"Me, too." I had a feeling I wouldn't be able to close my eyes without seeing the lifeless form of Angelina, Marlie-Beth, Zack, and that other kid for a while.

"Everything is becoming super intense," Remy said. "Do you think the commander is going to be able to keep you safe here? I mean, we are talking about the devil."

"Trev saw me, Remy," I heard myself saying. "And apparently, he is batting for the other team."

One perfect eyebrow arched. "Oh yeah? Well, I didn't see that one coming."

"None of us did." I paced the small dorm. My gut has never failed me. Not once had I viewed Trev as a threat. What was I missing? "Honestly, I still don't want to believe that Trev isn't my friend. He actually killed Angelina. Why would he do that if he was in their league?"

"I don't know, babe." She sat next to the sleeping Hannah. "We just need to be careful."

I loved how Remy said "we." It made me feel like I was part of a team. I wasn't alone in this.

I watched Remy curl up next to Hannah and doze off. My emotions were catching up with me. I had never witnessed someone dying, much less be the cause of them dying. No one had ever tried to murder me before, either.

I took a quick shower to try to erase the last couple of hours. Of course it didn't work. Then, after checking on my friends one more time and petting Champ, I crawled into bed and cried myself to sleep.

thirty-three

I SEARCHED FOR HIM IN my dreams, calling his name like it was a lifeline. One moment, I was walking barefoot in a tunnel that I had never seen before, and the next, I was standing in Finn's bedroom. He lay there with his hands crossed over his chest, his eyes twitching behind his closed lids. Whatever demons he faced were in his dreams.

I walked to the end of the bed and perched so close to him that I could have reached out and touched him. A familiar heat swirled in my belly. This was dream walking? What was I to do now?

I reached out to stroke the hair that had fallen over his eyebrows of its own volition. Before I touched his face though, he snagged my hand.

He didn't open his eyes as he asked, "You sought me out, Maka?" A smile lit his sleepy face.

"I didn't know that I could. I was upset before I went to sleep, and then I found myself here."

Green eyes flashed to mine as his grip tightened on me. "Dream walking uses a lot of power. I don't want you to draw more attention to yourself. Normally, I'd say no one could pick up on it while at the academy, but with Trev still missing …"

I swallowed nervously. "You think he knows I'm Nephilim?"

"I want to say no, but I'm no longer sure."

I sighed. "Why couldn't I have just been average?"

He smiled sleepily while he ran his thumb over my hand that he still held. "Nothing about you is average. He saw you take down Zack, but he has no clue who you really are. I'm scared we just whet his appetite. Hopefully, he doesn't know that Zack had just come into his powers and was immortal. That's what worries me the most. He would know exactly where the Flaming Sword is." He pulled me down on his chest. "Maka, I can feel the energy you are using from here. You need to return. I'll get dressed and come check on you."

"You don't have to do that." He looked so tired.

"It'd be my honor."

I gave a quick kiss and stood. Before I left though, I said, "I have one question, and then I'll go."

He put both hands behind his head. His muscles flexing made my mouth water. "Of course you do."

"I get that you can read my thoughts when I'm

broadcasting really loud, and I get that we are tied to each other's emotions now because of the bonding, but there has always been this feeling in the pit of my stomach. It's familiar, yet I can't label it. Do you know what it is?"

"That signature heat you feel in the pit of your stomach goes both ways. I feel it, too. I know when you are near, because you belong to me. You are my soulmate."

I was speechless for a second, letting my hands slowly fall to my sides. "Soulmate?"

He kicked the covers from him and stood slowly, revealing that he was in nothing other than a tight pair of black boxers. "Maka," he whispered, grabbing my arm and tugging me toward him, closing the distance between us. Then his lips crushed mine. This kiss was a kiss of a thousand stars that shone in the night sky. It was blinding and beautiful. Something to be treasured forever.

He gently pushed me away with a heavy sigh. "I need you to remember us, Maka." He gave me a tiny shove and, before I knew it, he was casting me out of his space.

I blinked and was back in the black tunnel, water rushing over my ankles. I should have been cold, but in my dream state, I found myself completely relaxed and comfortable. I knew the way back to my room, where I lay asleep, but I wanted answers. I was tired of living in a world where nothing made sense. I needed to put the pieces together before Camaella found her way to the academy, before Trev sold me out to whoever he was working for, and before more demons showed up.

All I had to do in my dream state was think of her, and I unfortunately found myself walking toward a scene that looked like a page from a horror film. I wasn't sure what state I was in, but the city was almost completely burned to the ground. One woman stood in the middle of the chaos, her red hair billowing behind her. With just a point of her finger, demons scrambled to do her bidding, killing everything in their path. Innocents were dying right in front of me. The carnage was like nothing I had ever seen.

The leader turned her head in my direction, giving me a smile that made me shake to the bone.

"Well, well, well, what do we have here, little dream walker?"

I gulped. "I, uh, I …"

She snapped her pearly white teeth together. "Cat got your tongue?" She started walking toward me.

This was a horrible idea. I needed to get back.

"Tell me, lovely, are you from the academy?"

"Um … no."

She stopped walking and cocked her head to the side. "Lies, but nice try."

Her red eyebrows rose. "You look just like Gabriel, you know. She always was such a beauty. A total bore, but she was blessed with unfathomable exquisiteness." She shook her head. "And now it's all coming back to me." She laughed crazily as I watched her tap a finger to her chin. "Those cheeky little archangels, always trying to pull a fast one on everybody. So, you didn't die that day, then?"

I had no clue what to say. I held my hands out to my side. "Well, I look alive, don't I?"

One side of her mouth lifted in a smirk. "That you do." She slipped her hands into the pockets of her sleek pantsuit. "You know I took no great joy in stabbing you on your wedding day."

I schooled my expression so that she wouldn't know that I was clueless. However, rage ran through me. So, this was the bitch that robbed me of a future.

"I'm sure," I seethed.

She took a couple of steps toward me. "How is that gorgeous commander?" She gave me a wink. "You have to be careful of guys like him. You know, the ones who have a touch of the devil in them." She laughed at me before shooing me along. "Go tell your Finn that I said I can't wait to see him again."

I turned to go.

"Oh, and lovely? You tell him that I said it will be really soon."

I fell into the tunnel, and the next thing I knew, Remy was shaking me awake. I was still in the same pajamas I went to sleep in, but my feet were wet from the tunnel. How could that be?

I couldn't breathe. Finn was going to be so mad when he realized what I had done.

thirty-four

WHEN THE WOLF STARTED GROWLING at the door, Remy gave me a look before she willed herself to become invisible. She shouted a warning at me to be careful before I opened it. Trev stood there with a backpack slung over his shoulders.

"We've got to go," he said, "and we have to go now."

I took a step back from him. "No, Trev, I'm not going anywhere with you."

As panic began to wrap its way around my heart, I felt the ball of yarn tighten. Finn would feel my panic and be here any second. I just had to stall.

Hannah sat up on the bed. "What's happening?"

"Some of Camaella's demon army has found the academy," Trev said. "There is a war going on."

I looked at my friends. "Shit. I think I alerted them. I

saw Camaella in a dream."

Trev grabbed my arm. "Hurry."

I jerked away from him. "We need to stay and fight," I said as I threw on clothes over my pajamas and laced up my boots.

"No, we don't."

I watched in horror as Trev brought up a gun. He fired off a shot at Hannah, who didn't even see it coming, and then he shot my beloved wolf.

Before I could turn, he placed the gun up to my neck and pulled the trigger.

"Relax, beautiful. It's just a tranquilizer dart. It will paralyze you, but it won't kill you." He swooped me up into his arms and began to jog down the hall.

Remy floated over to us. "I don't want him to know about me."

I tried to nod, but I couldn't get my head to move.

Trev stepped outside then ran through the courtyard, heading toward the woods when I realized something. There was no noise. None. Where was all the mayhem? Shouldn't there be demons running around, chasing terrified demis and the blessed? Obviously, Trev had lied about Camaella.

The trees surrounding us were blowing slightly in the night.

Trev smiled down at me as I lay limp in his arms. "You see that? Even with a dart in your system, you're still powerful. You're not a demi, Gabriella, and if you are not a demi, you are so much more. We have to get out of here."

Remy floated over to me. "What can I do?"

My eyes rolled over to her. It was the only way that I could let her know that I heard her.

"You have to be totally out of it before I bring you over," Trev said.

Over to where? my mind screamed.

I watched as Trev supported me with one arm. My legs hit the ground with a thud as he pulled out the dart gun and injected me again. My head lolled onto his shoulder.

So many things happened at once. Remy screamed, the binding around my heart tightened with rage, and Trev scooped me back up into his arms as he ran.

"Please know that I never meant to hurt you, Gabriella. In fact, just the opposite. From the bottom of my heart, I'm truly sorry."

I tried to scream but nothing came out. Instead, drool slipped past my lips and trailed down my chin. My head flopped as he picked up the pace, running through the woods.

Trev was crazy. I was in the arms of a madman. Whatever his agenda was, it was going to get us both killed.

The last image I had before I blacked out was one of Finn. He was going to be so mad at me when he found me. If he found me.

thirty-five

MAYBE BECAUSE I WAS TRANQUILIZED, or maybe because my heart knew what I needed, the archangels didn't come to me while I slept. In their place came a dream from a happier time. The day I was to be married.

My mother helped me dress in the most beautiful wedding dress that I had ever seen. All my aunts and uncles were coming for the big day. Aunt Ariel had given my future husband a ring just for me. It had been blessed, and I was currently wearing the engagement ring now. The emerald caught the rising light from the window just right and made me smile.

Mother fixed my hair with tears in her eyes. "You are lovely, daughter."

I gave her a hug before I stood and peeked out the window. "When will Finn be back?"

Mom laughed. "So anxious to get married, I see." She came

up behind me to look out the same window. "He ran to get something. It'll only take a few moments, darling daughter."

I knew what he had run to get. He thought he was so secretive, but I knew Finn like the back of my hand. He went back to the meadow that we loved to meet at. It held my favorite flower. He had mentioned today that no bride should go without a wedding bouquet. I had a feeling my charming soon-to-be husband went to fix that.

Chamuel came into our view. He was my favorite uncle. Not that I'd tell anyone that, but he loved to spoil me rotten. He was holding his belly, and there was a funny look on his face. Blood slowly started to seep through his fingers.

Not caring if I tore the train off my dress, I ran out the door, even as mother tried to hold me back.

He fell to his knees.

"Uncle," I screamed, "heal yourself."

"Can't," he gurgled.

There were screams and shouts coming from the barn that still adorned the simple wedding decorations. Uncle Sandalphon dragged a bleeding Raphael and Zadkiel over to my mother and I.

"Heal them," he shouted.

My mother dropped to her knees. She placed her palms on Zadkiel's stomach.

His blue eyes held regret. "The Flaming Sword did this."

"No, no, no!" I shouted. That meant their wounds were fatal. I was in shock as my mother still tried to heal her brother regardless of what information they just gave her. I dropped

to my knees beside her rocking as Uncle Uriel came up beside me, a wound gaping from his chest, I screamed. He was telling me to run. But run where? And without my family?

Mother was saying something to me, but I couldn't hear the words.

Giant wings soared above us. The commotion was growing louder and louder. I watched as the darken fought with the archangels. Uncle Jeremiel swung his sword cutting through one of the darken. It wasn't a killing blow because he didn't wield the Flaming Sword, but it would ensure that the darken wouldn't be getting up for the rest of the fight. A darken with red hair stalked towards me. Uncle Jeremiel went to intercept her but a darken stabbed him in the back. The red headed angel smiled as she sliced through my uncle. Sandalphon tackled her to the ground and then I lost them both as they chased one another. Uncle Jeremiel crawled toward me. Tears were streaming down my face as I looked at my uncles. Surely my mother could fix this.

More shouts were coming from the barn, the place that I was supposed to marry my love.

Mother stopped trying to heal Zadkiel. Why had she stopped? In a voice that I wasn't used to mother commanded her brothers that surrounded us.

"Their wounds are too deep," mother said with tears in her beautiful eyes. "We need to change our priorities."

They each placed their hands on me. A heat like no other radiated from their palms.

"What are they doing?" I asked Mother.

"Protecting you!" she shouted. Mom laid a warm hand on me, making me almost dizzy with the contact. She pointed at Haniel. "Stay here and guard her. I need to help Sandalphon push them back."

I was holding Chamuel's hand as he took his last breath.

I heard someone shout a moment before the redheaded darken appeared in front of me. Before I could blink, she swung a blade toward me. It cut right through my stomach. I watched as the blood seeped through the white wedding gown as I fell unto my back.

Haniel's scream was enough to make the ground quake.

I saw the beautiful red-haired angel sneer at me as I lay there in a pool of blood in the middle of my dead uncles, understanding that I would have the same fate as them.

In horror, I watched as the darken cut my grieving aunt down. As she fell, she grabbed my hand, pouring warm energy into me. She died clutching my wrist.

Knowing that I was dying, I watched the scene unfold around me with what little time I had left. The demons were dead, and it looked like the remaining archangels were defending as best as they could, but they couldn't kill them, not without the Flaming Sword that one of the darken were somehow wielding now.

I looked around at all the darken. They all had replicas of the Flaming Sword. The archangels were having a hard time pinpointing which was the real sword. This was planned.

Blood gurgled from my lips as I watched my mother take a cut to the lower abdomen. She stumbled over to me, half-

falling on top of me. I tried to stroke her hair, but my hands couldn't move.

Boots came into view. Then flowers. White peonies from the meadow where Finn and I loved to meet fell to the ground. My wedding bouquet.

I looked up into the most beautiful green eyes, wanting to tell him that I loved him, but no words came out.

His roar made my insides clench. Then he attacked the beautiful red-haired darken who held the Flaming Sword with such ferocity. She lost her hold on it after Finn broke her wrist, and he snatched the blade up.

The darken fell on him like a pack of wolves, but he never once lost the blade. My love had turned into a different person. He took out more darken than the archangels that were currently falling around me. I watched in amazement as the remainder took to the skies, retreating in defeat.

Blood covering him, he then knelt beside me as Azrael laid a hand on him. My love shrugged it off. "Heal her."

"You know that I can't. I can't heal any of them." Sadness was in his voice.

Finn tilted his head back and roared. "This is my fault. My father must have found out about the wedding."

Azrael shook his head. "We should have known better than to all congregate at one place like this, and it was I who got jumped by the lot of them. They got the sword because of me." He cleared his throat. "I can't heal her, but I could give her another chance at life."

Finn snarled, "Then do it."

Pain like no other radiated into me as Uncle Azrael chanted. I watched as the blade disappeared and poured into my soul.

My love dragged me out from under my mother and cradled me to his chest. His warm, spicy scent comforted me. Tears gathered in his beautiful green eyes.

I placed a bloody hand up to his face. I needed to tell him something one last time. "Finn, I love you."

"Maka"—he tightened his arms around me—"you will come back to me. Do you hear me? You must return. I am nothing without you."

Maka meant wife. Even though we hadn't made it to the ceremony, I knew that, in Finn's heart, that was exactly what I was. His wife.

My vision started to swim as I heard Azrael say, "She will come to you when the time is right."

"With her death, my father has killed us both."

I tried to speak again, but he laid a gentle finger to my lips. "Shh, sweetheart. It's all right. Everything is going to be fine."

I tried to give him a smile. He always did lie so well.

Azrael leaned down and brushed the hair from my face. My pain faded a bit. "I have given her an additional few minutes." He stood then, giving us privacy.

With new strength, I said, "Don't grieve too long for me. Promise me."

Tears rolled down his handsome face. "I will grieve for you until the day you come back to me."

"Tell me a story," I whispered.

"There once was a girl who held all the beauty in the world. Her smile was infectious to all. She was so pure because her heart was made of gold. Wherever she went, she brought a light with her that was so bright that it would chase the darkest shadows. My heart didn't beat until the day I first met her, and it will stop the day that I lose her, for she is my light, and I'm so afraid of the dark."

I took my last breath on that cold, dirt floor and, along with it, I took Finn's heart.

thirty-six

I AWOKE IN A CAVE. Trev had lit a fire and was warming some sort of meat over it.

My heart was raw with pain. Twice, in both my lives, I have found love and I have lost it. A long time ago, I had been about to marry Finn. He had loved me more than life itself. The girl who he had mourned was me.

I couldn't wait for him to save me. No, I had to save myself. I had to get back to Finn.

"Ah, you're awake," Trev said.

I rolled my head to look at him. "Let me go."

"Sorry, love. No can do. Sleep as much as possible, for tomorrow is a big day."

I tried to sit up, but I was too groggy. "What's tomorrow?"

A sad smile was plastered on his face while regret shone

in his eyes. "Don't worry, beautiful. I'm not taking you to the gates of hell. A close second, though. You are going to the Empowered Academy. Once there, you won't be allowed out without permission, and I have a feeling they won't be giving that anytime soon."

"Why?"

He knew exactly what I was asking.

"They want the commander to chase after you. He knows where the Flaming Sword is. It's the only thing that can kill an archangel or a darken. Without it, this war continues. Destruction will carry on until there is nothing left of the humans. I was sent to the academy to find Finn's weakness. You, beautiful, are that weakness. He will come for you, and I have a feeling he will finally tell us where that sword is."

"How?" I asked. "How could you betray me?"

"Easy, love. They have the twins."

"Your sisters?"

He nodded.

"Who has them?"

"The commander of the Empowered Academy."

He stared off into the fire. "I never meant to hurt you, Gabriella. Maybe that's the way it always goes, though. The archangels broke the rules, the darken were allowed to let demons roam, and then there's us—Nephilim, fully blessed, and demis fumbling around, determined to be on the right side, only to fall short."

My limbs were starting to feel less like Jell-O. I tried to

summon my power to me.

Trev sighed reluctantly as he pulled out the dart gun.

"No," I pleaded.

"Sorry, beautiful. If I don't get you to the academy, my sisters die."

I felt the pinch of the tranquilizer dart hit me in the neck. Tears fell down my face. My only saving grace now was keeping my secrets safe until I could escape. As long as they didn't know who I truly was, I should be relatively safe.

I felt the heaviness of my eyes as they began to close. Would I ever see Finn again?

CONTINUE THE STORY IN...

captured

special invitation

THREE SPECIAL INVITATIONS

1. I'd love to stay in touch with you and keep you updated about my new books! Join my newsletter to get all the latest information delivered straight to your inbox. Sign up at my website:

WWW.BRANDIELLEDGE.COM

2. Want to hang out with other readers who love my books? Join **BRANDI'S BOOK MAVENS** on Facebook and have fun with us. Oh yeah, I'll be there too!

3. Follow me on Instagram for cool giveaways! You can find me **@BRANDIELLEDGE**.

acknowledgements

THIS IS FOR THE FANTASTIC people in my life who I call family. You guys are a blessing. I thank God for each one of you every single day.

Matt, my hubby who gives me tacos. Cole and Caity for hands-down being the coolest kids ever. The year of double digits and teenagehood. Lord, help me.

Big shout out to Brook (with no e) and Martha Ann for being awesome beta readers.

Thanks, Rebecca, for going over the book even though I decided to do a complete re-do. It's just what crazy perfectionists do. Molly Phipps with "We Got You Covered" for the beautiful book cover. Kristin Campbell for taking this baby and making it shine. Michelle Bryan, for your advice.

Love you all.

about the author

BRANDI ELLEDGE lives in the South, where even the simplest words are at least four syllables.

She has a husband that she refused to upgrade…because let's face it he is pretty awesome, and two beautiful children that are the light of her life.

Find her online at:

WWW.BRANDIELLEDGE.COM

Made in the USA
San Bernardino, CA
18 July 2020